DRAGON RIDERS

DAPHNE ASHLING PURPUS

ISBN: 061565777X
ISBN-13: 9780615657776
Library of Congress Control Number: 2012911805
Purpus Publishing, Vashon, WA

DEDICATION

This novel is dedicated to the real dragon riders: those who work everyday to banish hatred and discord from our world.

CONTENTS

ACKNOWLEDGMENTS

I have been helped, inspired, and supported by so many people as I worked to fulfill my dream of writing a novel. First, I'd like to thank the folks at National Novel Writing Month (NaNoWriMo) for all their encouragement and pep talks. I completed the first draft of *Dragon Riders* in November of 2011.

Next, I'd like to thank the members of my Wednesday Bridge Class who have been unfailing in their support of my efforts: Blythe Bartlett, Jude Boardman, Tink Campbell, Edna Dam, Jim Dam, Beth de Groen, Barbara Garrison, Billie Hendrix, JoAnn Nielsen, Janet Quimby, Julia Rhoads, Peg Rider, Jerry Snell, Sharon Staehli, Ellen Trout, and Carolyn Youngblood.

I would also like to thank my students, both past and present, at Student Link, Vashon's alternative high school, who continue to inspire me with their drive, determination, maturity, and insight in the face of major adversities—the real dragon riders.

I would like to thank my editors at CreateSpace, without whom this novel would never have been published, and extra thanks to my main editor, Lindsey.

And finally, many thanks—in no particular order—to Cynthia Zheutlin for her gentle wisdom, Kelly Wright for her caring knowledge, Amber Starcher for her cheerful helpfulness, Kay

Farris for her friendship and support, Trevor Tuma for his kindness and delicious kale chips, Connie Gaut for her efficiency and enthusiasm, Nell Coffman for her support of me and my four-legged companions, Lydia Schoch for her empathy and wisdom, Peter Scott for his interest and encouragement, Nan Hammett for her friendship and collegial support, Kathy Wheaton for her friendship, and Anja Moritz for her wisdom, kind support, and wonderful lunches.

PROLOGUE

Elfrik woke from his dream sleep and turned quickly to check on his dragon, Sophia, as well as his other dragon riders and their dragons. He noticed that Edmund, his second in command, was stirring and the others seemed to be about ready to awaken.

Elfrik looked around to see where they had landed. Dream travel had proven to be a life saver for the dragons and their riders over the centuries, but it was very disorienting. The destination was never known to the riders. However, as far as Elfrik knew from his study of the dragon riders' chronicles, dream travel had never harmed them.

Elfrik saw that they had landed in a large mostly flat grassy field, and as he stood he noticed several things at once. There were three people, a gryphon, and a unicorn approaching them and nearby a horse was grazing. In the distance to the south Elfrik could see a fishing village and off to the west there were fields with crops of some sort. But Elfrik quickly brought his attention back to the approaching delegation.

The tallest of the three people spoke first. "Greetings, travellers," he said. "Welcome. I am King Stephen and you have landed in my country called Sanwight. I would like to introduce my fellow rulers. On my left is King Eric and his co-ruler the

Gryphon Corbin They rule the land of Forbury. And on my right is Queen Pamela and her co-ruler, the Unicorn Serafina, who rule the nation of Granvale. Our world is comprised of just three nations and when we heard your telepathic calls, we set out to welcome you. My co-ruler is a dolphin named Clarice and you will be able to hear her telepathically I am sure and hopefully meet her in person if you decide to stay in our world.

King Eric then said, "Yes, welcome to our world and may we ask what has brought you here. We have been watching over you and yours since you appeared on our world three days ago."

Elfrik, who realized his mouth was gaping and his eyes were wide with astonishment, pulled himself together. He shook his head to try to clear it and as he was doing so he heard a voice speaking to him telepathically. *Are you surprised to find more telepathic beings, dragon rider? Have you never encountered any other species who was telepathic?*

Elfrik realized it was Corbin talking with him and he enjoyed the communication with wonder, noticing his fellow dragons and dragon riders reacting similarly. Elfrik spoke, "We are so pleased with your welcome. We have had to leave our homes after our former world turned against dragons and riders. We are a peace-loving people, riders and dragons alike, and all we ask for is a place which we can make our own. We are most willing to help others in any way that we can."

Queen Pamela spoke for the first time. She was shorter than the two men, but equally regal in bearing. She had long flowing white hair and startling blue eyes. She asked, "Why did your world turn against you?"

Elfrik, a very tall skinny man in his mid-forties with brown hair, greying at the temples, and deep brown eyes, thought for a moment before replying. "Centuries ago, when our ancestors first arrived on our last world, they were welcomed. No one else on that world was either telepathic or capable of forming symbiotic bonds with other species. Nevertheless, they were welcoming. However, over the years, people started to envy and fear the dragons and their riders. They couldn't understand the nature of telepathy and they saw the dragons not as intelligent beings but rather as threats. They knew that dragons can breathe fire, for instance, but they refused to believe that dragons are at heart a peace-loving race. So in their greed and fear and ignorance they decided that dragon eggs could be stolen, that dragons should be hunted for their beautiful scales, that dragons should be captured and put on display at circuses and the like."

Elfrik continued, "As you might imagine, our numbers dropped dramatically. Female dragons won't lay eggs if they are stressed and many of those which were laid turned out to be deformed or unable to hatch. What you see before you," he said as he gestured around him to about thirty riders and dragons, "is all that is left of our people. We have barely enough to start again. This has happened to us in the past, according to our chronicles, and whenever our numbers reach a critical point, we are sent into a dream travel state where we are brought to a new world to start over. We arrive unconscious and sleep for about three days as our bodies readjust to the travel, or so our chroniclers have written. If we are in danger during that time, we can awaken, but it is not easy, so we are most grateful that you allowed us to continue the process at our natural pace."

King Eric, a tall handsome young man with blond hair and blue eyes and a slender build, answered Elfrik. "On our world, as you have discovered, you will not be alone in either forming a symbiotic relationship with another species, or in being able to communicate telepathically. If our world suits you, you will find allies, and over all, as I think my fellow rulers will concur, our nations function well with both telepaths and non-telepaths." The others nodded in agreement.

Corbin spoke aloud. "You will find, Elfrik, that gryphons, and unicorns are able to use human speech when necessary."

All of a sudden they all heard Clarice telepathically. *I do hope you are not making any snide comments about dolphins not speaking in human speech.* But they also heard the giggle in her thoughts and knew she wasn't serious.

Serafina spoke next saying, "Of course not, Clarice, and after all you are the only one who survives in our oceans, so you hold a special place in our world, as indeed we all do.

King Stephen concurred. "I think, Elfrik, that what we are all trying to say is that our individual nations are quite different but that we try to treat everyone with respect, riders, and non-riders alike. And as luck would have it, about one fourth of our world is uninhabited. I'm not sure if it will suit you, but do you see that volcanic mountain off to the north?"

Elfrik nodded and King Stephan continued. "Our world has been divided into the three existing nations, as we mentioned. King Eric and Corbin rule over Forbury which is south of here. It is a heavily forested mountain region, specializing in mining and lumbering. Queen Pamela and Serafina rule over Granvale, west of here, specializing in farming. And finally, Clarice and I rule over Sanwight which is a nation of fishermen and related industries. But as I mentioned, the volcanic mountainous region to the north is uninhabited. Would this type of terrain interest you?"

Elfrik looked at his dragons and riders. He spoke telepathically to both Sophia, his gorgeous purple dragon, and Edmund. *What say you? Do you think this is a good place?*

They both nodded and Sophia noted, *Our chronicles never mention us finding a world where telepaths already existed, so I think this is a very good omen.*

Elfrik looked back at the other rulers and said, "If you will accept us, we would be happy to settle here. Since dragons love heat, living around a volcano would suit us very nicely and we could even work at harnessing the volcano's energies for use by all nations, releasing the pent up energies slowly and uniformly so that the volcano remains dormant."

Queen Pamela said, "That would be much appreciated. I'm afraid if the volcano were to erupt it would damage much of our world."

King Eric nodded and went on. "You have arrived in our land at a most propitious time. All three of our nations are preparing for the birthing and bonding ceremonies for the next generation of riders. If you would like to accompany us, you could see for yourselves first hand what our world is like. At the same time, the rest of your group is welcome to remain here and food and any other necessities will be provided for you. How does that seem?"

"That sounds wonderful," answered Elfrik. "Sophia and I would be happy to accompany you. Edmund, can you set up camp here? I will stay in touch telepathically with you and relate what we see." Edmund nodded.

"Excellent," replied King Stephen. "Well this will be exciting for you, I hope. This afternoon we will watch the dolphins birthing and bonding with our new riders. Tomorrow we are off to Granvale to see the unicorn ceremony, and finally, on the third day we will watch the gryphon bondings. These ceremonies are ancient and sacred, and I'm sure you and your dragons have something similar. Shall we leave for my palace and once there I will be sure you have time to eat and bathe before the ceremony begins."

After a brief ride the group arrived at King Stephen's palace and Elfrik and Sophia were very grateful for the reception they were accorded. Soon it was time for the ceremony. Corbin, Serafina, and Sophia stayed in the palace gardens, participating tele-pathically with their respective riders, as King Stephen took King Eric, Queen Pamela, and Elfrik down through a long pas-sageway to a grotto underneath the palace. When they arrived there, Elfrik marveled at the beauty of the spot. There were detailed mosaics all around the grotto showing what Elfrik assumed to be the history of the dolphins and their riders. However, his attention immediately turned to the large pool in the center of the grotto, a pool, Elfrik quickly realized, that was merely an extension of a large stream entering the grotto.

Elfrik noticed that there were nine dolphins in the water along with about fifteen swimmers, children about twelve years old, Elfrik guessed. Soon the birthing began. As the dolphins, one by one, gave birth to newborn dolphins, the children waited along the edge of the pool in eager anticipation. Elfrik was fas-cinated to see that the newborn dolphins swam away from their mothers and headed toward one of the children. Some-times the newborn made a direct beeline for a particular child and sometimes they swam around a bit, apparently searching, before choosing a rider. In every case, as soon as the child was chosen by a dolphin the child held onto the dolphin and called aloud to let everyone know what the newborn's name was. It was a very magical process, and Elfrik was rather overwhelmed by it all. It was similar in many ways to what the dragons did when they hatched, but in other ways it was distinctly different.

Elfrik kept describing everything he saw to Sophia, and he felt her joy and happiness at witnessing such a magnificent sight. The new riders and dolphins were escorted out of the grotto and soon it was only the spectators left. Those children who were not chosen were being consoled by their parents and friends who had been watching the ceremony, and soon every-one filed out of the grotto to join in a feast in the palace to celebrate the new bondings. The feast was held in the garden and Elfrik and Sophia were soon being introduced to many new faces. King Stephen seemed to realize just when this was more than Elfrik and Sophia could handle on their first day in this world, and he graciously whisked them away to an area where they could relax and sleep.

The next day, Elfrik and the three monarchs traveled to Granvale and again, Elfrik was amazed by the splendor of the palace. He and Sophia realized that this world contained the proud heritage of many groups. Today's ceremony was held in the unicorn rider's village near the palace. There was a special large corral where the female unicorns who were ready to birth were relaxing. And again, around the edge of the corral on the inside, were a group of twelve to fifteen year old children, eager and hopeful. There were seats outside the corral for parents, friends and of course the monarchs, and there was even a special section reserved for Corbin, Serafina, and now Sophia. As each new unicorn was born, its mother licked the new colt clean and then stepped back as the baby unicorn staggered to one of the eager rider candidates. It never failed to amaze Elfrik, as it did with dragon hatchings, that the newborn was able to find just the right rider with little or no hesitation. He did feel sorry for those who weren't chosen, but that was the way of the world.

Finally on the third day they arrived in Forbury. The setup for the gryphon birthing was understandably similar to that of the unicorns. This time there were twelve gryphons ready to birth and about twenty young people, Elfrik guessed because before he could get an accurate count, the first gryphon had gone into labor and the excitement mounted. Once all twelve gryphons had successfully given birth to twelve gawky but healthy newborns, all of whom had found their own rider, the party headed off to the palace for the final celebrations.

By the end of three days of birthings, bondings, and celebrations, Elfrik and Sophia were exhausted and ready to get back to their own family. There was one last meeting with King Eric, Queen Pamela, and King Stephen where a large map of the world was displayed and Elfrik was shown where his new nation of Draconia would be situated. The other monarchs stressed the importance of having a bonded monarchy to rule each of the nations and Elfrik and Sophia were sure that their riders would consent to his becoming King Elfrik. He and Sophia would rule over Draconia, and hopefully the new location would allow the population of dragons and riders to grow again.

— 1 —
EGG LAYING

The sun shone bright on a hot summer day as the male dragons of Draconia circled overhead in the clear blue sky. Every color of the rainbow was present—blues, greens, browns, reds, oranges, yellows, and the most powerful, but very rare, purple dragons. All their eyes were focused below on the sand pit that shimmered in the heat.

This pit had been built five hundred years ago when the dragon riders arrived in Draconia. It was a large sand pit surrounded by a four foot high, six foot thick, stone wall, lavishly carved by early stone masons to portray the long and powerful tradition of dragons and their riders. But today was not the day for reading or admiring the walls. Today was the summer solstice when the egg-laying female dragons would lay their eggs, and so the focus of all the dragons was on that most important task. Dragons mated for life. They were fiercely loyal to their mates, but the actual mating ritual only occurred every three years.

A dragon can mate with any color dragon, but the offspring were always the same color as the mother. Today's thirteen females consisted of two blues, two greens, one brown, three reds, two oranges, two yellows, and one purple—Matilda, the leader of the dragons.

As the sun reached its noontime high, the male dragons cried out in unison as the female dragons entered the sand pit, accompanied by their riders. The pit was large enough to accommodate all thirteen females without crowding. All the other riders watched from the wall as the dragons walked around the pit, each encouraged by her rider, looking for the ideal location to lay her egg. Matilda and her rider, Clotilda, leader of the dragon riders, naturally got the first pick of location. Matilda chose the very center.

Once all the female dragons were satisfied with their spot in the pit, each began to prepare the spot for her egg. The dragon riders helped and soon shallow depressions had been made to house the eggs. Draconia's volcano provided the heat necessary to keep the sands warm and the eggs properly incubated. Over the years, dragon riders had channeled the hot sulfur springs so that they flowed right beneath the sand, ensuring that it was always warm and ready.

Clotilda—a tall woman in her late forties with short, grey hair and wire-framed glasses—kept in constant telepathic communication with Matilda, as did the other riders with their dragons, encouraging and sending loving thoughts toward the dragons as they prepared to lay their eggs. This was a very magical moment that had been celebrated for as long as anyone could remember.

The first dragon to lay an egg was Brunhilda, a lovely brown-mottled dragon, and the youngest of the laying dragons. This was her first egg laying. Her mate, Rothgar, soared around the pit, diving and swooping, performing all sorts of outrageous maneuvers, whooping, yelling, and sending out long flames. Brunhilda smiled up at him as Cyrus, Brunhilda's rider, checked telepathically and found that the egg was perfect with a healthy brown dragon inside. Cecil, Rothgar's rider, shook hands with everyone around him as if he'd done something spectacular. It was comical to watch, but it really took all four—two dragons and two riders—to bring an egg laying to a successful conclusion. The female laid the egg, then the riders of both dragons had to care for it in the pit, rotating it every few hours, and watching for any signs of difficulty. Dragons were not very maternal by nature, and without the riders' help, the species would probably have died out.

One by one, the dragons released their eggs into their shallow depressions as the riders connected with the eggs to be sure that they were alive and healthy. Matilda was the last dragon to deposit her egg as her mate, Maurice, and his rider, Hamlet, looked on. Once the egg was safely in the sand, Clotilda verified that there was a healthy, purple, female dragon inside the light-purple egg. Clotilda then congratulated Matilda, both of them feeling a sense of pride and a pang of sadness ,as they knew this was probably Matilda's last egg-laying. Her days of fertility were drawing to a close.

As the egg laying ceremony ended, the male dragons landed around the pit to watch over the eggs as the females returned to their caves with their riders for a well earned rest. The dragon riders who had been observing broke out in thunderous applause, celebrating the fact that all thirteen dragons had laid perfect eggs. Now it was their turn to watch over and carefully turn the dragon eggs as needed.

A couple of dragon riders, Hans and Jake , who were also brothers, came up to Cecil to congratulate him and then teased him. Hans said, "Now that you are on egg duty, we'll have to take over your regular duties I suppose."

Jake continued, "You don't think Draconia will take care of itself while you are here turning your egg, do you?"

Cecil grinned. This was the first mating for his Rothgar and Brunhilda, and he was as proud as he could be. "Don't worry," he countered. "One day, Hans, it will be your turn when your lovely Fire Dancer takes a mate, and you, too, Jake, when Harmony finds her match."

Hans laughed. "You are right. Truly, Jake and the other riders and I are happy to take over your duties away from Havenshold. We all know how important it is to the continuation of the species to have many successful hatchings, so no worries. Besides, once Brunhilda's egg has hatched, you can pay us back!"

Cecil smirked. "Don't count on it!"

Meanwhile, Clotilda accompanied Matilda back to their cave and made sure she was comfortable in her nest. Each dragon and rider had their own cave carved out of the side of the volcanic mountain. Each had equipped it according to their own personal tastes and needs. Both Clotilda and Matilda favored purple, so there was a lovely purple quilt in Matilda's nest and an identical one on Clotilda's bed. A large water bowl filled one of the niches and another had some dragon treats as well as human snacks. Clotilda made sure that Matilda had everything she needed. She oiled Matilda's scales with a lovely lavender-scented oil made especially for dragon hides. All the time that Clotilda did this, she stayed in telepathic contact with Matilda, letting her know that she was the most wonderful of all the dragons. The two of them had been bonded for nearly forty years, and there was nothing that they didn't know about each other.

Matilda was becoming drowsy as Clotilda rubbed the oil in. She turned over so Clotilda could get her belly, and as she did so she mused, "I wonder who our egg will pick as her rider."

Clotilda answered, "I've been watching all the potential candidates closely. There is a fine group of twelve to fourteen year olds to chose from. I know you dragons have been doing the same thing. Is there anyone special you have your eye on?"

Matilda grew coy. "I was thinking about someone. Can you guess?"

Clotilda laughed. "You can't fool me. I think that Emily—Hans and Jake's sister—would be perfect."

Matilda pretended to pout. "However did you guess? Oh, could you rub more oil into my arm pits, please?"

"Sure," said Clotilda, smiling. "It wasn't hard to guess. She is a natural leader and she comes from a family strong in the dragon tradition. I think she would be a perfect choice, but then, we both know that it isn't up to us."

"I know," said Matilda sleepily. She rolled over to nap. Clotilda yanked her quilt off her bed and curled up with Matilda as they had done so many times before.

Just as Clotilda thought Matilda was asleep, Matilda surprised her by asking, "Do you regret never finding a mate?"

"Not really," answered Clotilda. "Or, at least, not most of the time. I know you and Maurice enjoy your time together, and Maurice has a great dragon rider in Hamlet, but neither Hamlet nor I have ever found kindred spirits. Honestly, with you as my companion, I have all I need. Besides which, being leader of the dragon riders is a full time job. I don't really have time for anyone but you."

Matilda chuckled. "We do make a good team, don't we?" With that comment she began to snore. The wall hangings shook from the vibrations, and as Clotilda started to drift off to sleep, she thought she could feel contented snores throughout Havenshold.

It had been a very successful day. All thirteen dragons had laid viable eggs. Now there was nothing to do but wait and carefully tend the eggs. In six months, at the winter solstice, there would be a hatching, and new baby dragons would bond with their chosen riders.

— 2 —
HISTORY LESSON

Emily watched the dust motes dancing in the sunlight that streamed through her classroom window as she fiddled with one of her long brown braids. It was a lovely autumn day, and she was daydreaming about being outside, watching the dragons soar across the blue sky. She wasn't particularly interested in this morning's history class, which seemed to be filled with nothing but dates. She looked across the classroom at her best friend, Anne, who was doodling in her book and didn't seem any more engaged in the lesson than she was.

Both girls were twelve-years-old and came from families of dragon riders. Emily had two older brothers, Jake and Hans, who had been selected by dragons. Jake was bonded with a beautiful brown dragon named Harmony. Emily remembered that Jake had been a very active twelve-year-old five years ago. He had gotten into more trouble than their parents thought possible. The family stories about Jake's escapades were legend. His biggest coup had been to set all the riders' sheep loose in the middle of the night. It had taken several days to get them all rounded up, but Jake had changed after he bonded with Harmony. Now he was Emily's favorite brother.

Emily's other dragon-riding brother, Hans, was bonded with a bright orange dragon named Fire Dancer. Together, they frequently won the dragon competitions for acrobatics. Emily didn't really remember Hans as a boy, since he was ten years older, but she was proud of him now, even if he had no time for his little sister.

Emily's parents were both retired riders. In fact, her family could trace their lineage back five hundred years to King Elfrik, who brought the dragons and riders to this world. Emily was one of six children, and she was the third to be selected to attend a hatching. She couldn't wait for the next fortnight to pass. She was excited, nervous, and scared all at the same time, and that made concentrating on her blasted history lesson all the harder.

Anne's parents were also both retired riders. Anne—as the oldest child in her family—was the first to be selected as a rider candidate. The girls spent hours talking about the hatching and wondering which egg might hatch a dragon they would like, before they realized that the important thing was whether the dragon liked them. Both Anne and Emily had been attending hatchings as spectators since they were very young, but since the hatchings only happened every three years, the girls really only had a good memory of the last one they'd seen when they were nine.

It was hard to see everything from the spectator's seats, which were high above the hatching pit floor, but they remembered the sad faces on those who weren't chosen, especially those who were attending for their second time since they knew it was their last chance. You were rarely allowed two chances. If—as was the case with Anne and Emily—you were barely twelve when you were at your first hatching, then you would be allowed to attend again in three years if you didn't get selected. However, if you were thirteen or fourteen, one shot was all you got.

Two of Emily's other classmates were also dragon rider candidates for this year's hatching—Joseph and William. Emily liked them both, although they didn't give her the time of day. *Boys,* she thought, *are nearly as strange as dragons.*

Emily's ears perked up. The teacher, Miss Raven, was talking about the founding of Draconia by the early dragons and riders following the Dragon Wars. This was history Emily could pay attention to. After all, it was her family's history as well. Miss Raven explained how their world was originally divided into three countries, with the mountainous region remaining uninhabited. The other three nations—Sanwight on the ocean, Granvale in farming country, and Forbury, inland with forests and gold mines—didn't care about the high craggy mountainous region in the center of the land. They were also leery of the volcano, which spurted flames occasionally. But that was the perfect spot for the dragon riders who had arrived by dream travel five hundred years ago.

And so, Miss Raven continued, "Draconia became the fourth nation in our world. The dragons and riders were good to their word. The volcano, while still active, has provided a source of heat and healing hot springs that all the nations can enjoy. The dragon riders elected Elfrik and Sophia as their first bonded monarchs. As the dragons and their riders settled into their new homes, harmony returned. Slowly, the dragon population grew. The dragon riders married, had children, and the population of Draconia grew. Some riders chose to leave active duty while they raised their children. Not all children were selected to be riders, so other groups grew into the society, which is why today we have barons, farmers, artisans, craftsmen, and many others. Our land is not as productive as, say, Granvale, but we manage to raise our sheep, cattle, and goats not only to feed the dragons, but to feed ourselves as well. All four nations have trade agreements, so that, for example, the fish from Sanwight get traded for grain and produce in Granvale, and wood and gold in Forbury, and power and hot springs from our Draconia. Our mountainous terrain and lack of roads make this challenging, but the magical creatures ensure that trading continues.

"The dragons also serve to patrol the skies and watch the borders, not only to ensure peace between the nations, but also to be prepared for incursions from other worlds. We want our way of life to continue where bonds with magical creatures are honored and treasured."

At that moment, the bell rang and class was over for the day. Emily and Anne raced out the door, saying goodbye before each headed to her respective home and afternoon chores.

"See you later!" called Emily.

"Right!" answered Anne.

— 3 —

DRAGON HATCHING

Emily woke up before sunrise. She was very excited and very scared. It was the winter solstice, the holiest day of the year, and one that was always wonderful. But this solstice was the *most important one in her life,* and would determine the course her life would take. Today was the dragon hatching.

Emily remembered when her parents had told her she'd been selected. Nearly a month ago her dad had called her into the kitchen where her mother was. He said, "The dragons have made their selection for candidates for this hatching."

Emily waited, shifting from foot to foot. Neither of her parents was smiling. She wanted to be a dragon rider more than anything in the whole world. That meant she had to be selected as a candidate, as her older brothers had been. How could she be a dragon rider if she weren't a candidate? Finally she could stand the suspense no longer. "Well?" she shouted. "Who got chosen?"

Her mother said, "Gregory, of course. His father, Baron Geldsmith, made such a *stink* about Gregory not being chosen by a dragon at the last hatching that the dragons *had* to include him again. Funny, I don't think Gregory's that interested, but his father is, and his father is the most *powerful* baron in the country."

"OK," said Emily, waving her hand as if batting a fly. "But who are the others?"

Her father answered, "Joseph and William were chosen, and Anne. There are twenty candidates this time for the thirteen eggs."

Emily could stand it no longer. "Was I picked?" she wailed. She couldn't tell if her parents were teasing her and deliberately prolonging her agony, or if they were trying to let her down gently.

Her parents burst into big smiles. Her mother said, "Yes, dear! You were!"

Emily thought that had been about the best moment in her life. The past month had been a whirlwind of activities to get ready for today. She'd been fitted for the special white candidate's robe. She'd been instructed in how to fix a dragon's first meal. She'd learned where to sit, and how to sit, and a million other things she couldn't even think of now. But finally, the day had come.

Emily raced down to the kitchen to find her parents already there. This was a big day for them as well. She was the third in her family to become a dragon rider candidate, and she fervently hoped she would soon be the third *chosen.* Emily got to work preparing a dragon breakfast. It had to be fresh, she had to do all the preparations herself, and she had to have it ready to take to the hatching ceremony in two hours.

Emily remembered all the instructions about having fresh meat and cutting the pieces into one inch cubes so the baby dragon could swallow without choking. She had to mix in some vegetables and make lots of tasty gravy as well. There was a basic hatching breakfast recipe, but her family had modified it. They had their own secret formula, and now Emily knew that secret.

The two hours flew by. Emily was freshly bathed, robed in her candidate's robe, and headed to the hatching pit with her dragon's breakfast safely stowed in a container with hot stones to keep it warm. Her parents walked with her. Soon, they met up with Anne and her family, and then Joseph, William, and their families. The four of them had already decided to sit together at the hatching, and their families would be anxiously watching from the spectator's gallery high above.

Emily's brothers would be there as well, but they would be with their dragons supervising the hatching to be sure no one approached the eggs and that no one was hurt.

All too soon, the candidates were seated cross-legged in the sand around the edge of the hatching pit. Emily understood why they had to have special robes, as the sand was very hot. The robes were like giant pot-holders and protected them from burning. A hush settled over the stadium as everyone waited.

First, a brown dragon egg cracked, and the dragon began working its way out of the shell. This was a very tense moment for everyone, because it wasn't easy to crack a dragon egg. This was the first test for the baby dragon. Not all dragons managed to hatch successfully—that meant they weren't strong enough to live.

Emily thought that they should be helped, but that was forbidden. Better that the dragon die than a weakling be born.

But, today was a lucky day for the new baby brown as it managed a successful hatching. It wobbled unsteadily on its legs, lurching around, trying to get its wings unstuck from egg fluid. The candidates had been instructed that they were not allowed to move or try to entice the dragon in any way. The dragon had to find its new rider all by itself. The bond between dragon and rider was incredibly strong, but only because it was a mutual bond, one the dragon and rider freely entered into. Emily had never heard of a rider not accepting a dragon, but in theory they could. The dragon had to make the choice first.

The baby brown staggered for a few more minutes, and then, in a comical lurching gate, made its way directly for William. William almost forgot his part as he was so surprised, but after Joseph and Anne nudged him, he quickly brought out the dragon breakfast and started hand-feeding his new dragon. All of a sudden, William looked up and said, "His name is Thunder! I can hear him talking in my head!" Loud applause rose from the spectators. William and Thunder were escorted out of the hatching pit and into the dragon riders' quarters.

Attention quickly turned back to the hatching pit.

Emily and Anne whispered to each other that they thought it was a good sign that William got picked first. He was a good friend. It'd been a surprise to both girls that William had been chosen as a candidate, since he was very shy and quiet—a towheaded boy, tall and skinny, who seemed to have trouble *not* tripping over his feet. But as Emily had been told so many times, dragons saw right into the very *heart* of a person. They knew more than the person knew about himself. The dragons had been right in making William a candidate.

Now the hatching moved on with greater speed as several eggs started hatching at once. *Please, please pick me,* thought Emily, over and over again. Three other candidates were picked by a baby green, a baby blue, and a baby red. Then, Anne was chosen. An ungainly looking yellow came staggering over to Anne, and Anne cooed with delight. As she opened her dragon breakfast to feed her new friend, she announced, "Her name is Samantha!"

Emily started to worry. She, along with the other candidates, had helped maintain the hatching grounds, and so she also had touched and rolled all the eggs. Of course, she didn't have a favorite. She'd be thrilled with any of the dragons. They were all magnificent creatures. Secretly, though, she thought that the purple egg was the prettiest, but she wouldn't breathe a word of that to anyone.

Now there were only three eggs left and ten candidates. Joseph had been selected a few minutes ago—by a baby green named Spruce—and so now Emily was sitting by herself with her three friends already off in the dragon riders' quarters.

Emily looked around the pit and caught Gregory looking at her from across the circle. He smiled at her and she smiled back. She'd always liked Gregory, even if his father was a jerk. You couldn't help who your parents were. Emily knew she was really lucky to have such wonderful parents, and while she and her five brothers and sisters were very different, they all loved each other. Gregory was not so lucky. His father was a jerk on a power trip, and his younger brother teased him and made his life a nightmare. Gregory's mother had died when his brother was born, so Gregory was alone. Emily couldn't imagine what that might feel like. She smiled again at Gregory before looking down at the eggs.

What? thought Emily. *There's only one egg left—the purple—and it hasn't even started to hatch. What if it's a weakling and can't hatch?*

A hush fell over the stadium and everyone watched. What seemed like years was really only minutes. There was a loud crack and the entire egg burst apart. No other dragon baby had managed that. Every other hatching had been a slow and laborious process of widening the hole until the dragon could stagger out, but not this time. The egg looked as if it had exploded and a magnificent purple dragon appeared—a bit ungainly, to be sure, but definitely confident.

There were still eight candidates around the pit. Emily couldn't help but think that her chances were slim, but she didn't have long to think that. Without a second's hesitation, the baby purple made a beeline for Emily, moving with only minor staggering. There was no looking around, no pauses to think, the dragon just headed right to her. Emily could hear the dragon talking in her head before they even touched. *I am Esmeralda,* the dragon announced.

Emily quickly got out her dragon breakfast. As she fed Esmeralda from her hands, she though, *How different my life will be now. Esmeralda looked up at her and said,* Yes, it will be different for both of us.

— 4 —

RIDER EDUCATION

Emily was absolutely exhausted. She couldn't remember ever having worked so hard and slept so little in her life. To think that one month ago she had been worried about whether she would be picked by a dragon, and now she could barely move. The life of a dragon rider was a lot tougher than she'd imagined. Esmeralda needed constant attention. She reminded Emily of her youngest siblings when they were first born.

As tired as she was, Emily was overjoyed to have bonded with Esmeralda, who had grown at an astonishing rate! She had been only about a foot long when she was born, but now in just one month, she was over four feet long! No more cooking breakfasts with one-inch cubes. Instead Emily had to help Esmeralda catch her own breakfast—starting with small rodents and working her way up to larger prey—and she had to harvest the fruit and veggies to go with the raw meat.

Then there was the *constant* skin care. Emily was taught how to oil Esmeralda after rubbing her down with sand—something Esmeralda just delighted in, insisting that Emily use the lavender scented oil as that was her favorite. Esmeralda didn't like being alone and she wanted Emily with her at all times.

Dragons didn't need nearly as much sleep as twelve-year-old girls did.

Emily rarely saw her friends. Sometimes she ran into Anne, Joseph, or William when she was hunting for Esmeralda's food or getting more oil, but there was no time to chat. Her friends looked just as tired and harried as she did. *Babies of any species are a handful,* Emily decided. Dragons were the smart ones, handing the raising of their offspring to the humans.

The older riders mentored the new riders. Each had a teacher to help them learn about dragon care and what needed to be done to raise a dragon properly, but the mentors were not allowed to *help* in any way. The actual care had to be done by the dragon rider, as that was how their bond was strengthened.

Emily couldn't believe how smart Esmeralda was and how much they loved each other. Esmeralda was rather selfish and self-centered, but she *was* only a baby. A baby's world revolved around them and only them, but she was not mean-spirited, and she was always happy to see Emily and eager to learn new things.

By the time Esmeralda was six-months-old, she was almost full-size. She was nearly fifteen feet long from head to tail. Her wings were a radiant, iridescent purple, while her body was a deeper richer purple. She wouldn't reach her final height of over ten feet and wing span of at least twenty feet until she was a year old, and then it would take another couple years before she gained enough strength to fly more than short distances. She would be six-years-old before she could carry a rider, but Emily could wait. She had her own growing up to do.

At six months, dragons were able to be left on their own for a few hours at a time. This was when the dragon riders returned to the classroom. Education was taken very seriously in Draconia. If Emily hadn't been selected as a dragon rider, by age thirteen she would have had to pick a profession and begin preparing for it. Having been selected meant the decision of a career was solved for her, but her education had just begun.

"Why are we back in a classroom?" Emily asked as she, Anne, Joseph, William, and the other new riders headed off to the large building in the center of the dragon rider's complex.

"I don't know," answered Joseph, who had always felt that school was a waste of time. He loved to read, but preferred learning on his own. "Haven't we been learning enough from our mentors?"

"I could use a *very* long nap," said Anne, running her fingers through her short blond hair. "Samantha's kept me *really* busy! I know school's important, but right now I have more than enough just keeping up with Samantha."

"Yeah," said William, who usually was quiet. "Thunder lives up to his name. He snores so loudly, *I* can't sleep! And he wants me to sleep curled up with him so I also shake as his snores rock everything in our cave!"

The others laughed, but agreed that some time off would be nice. They reached the classroom, entered, and found seats. Soon, one of the senior dragon riders—Hamlet—came in to begin class. Hamlet was bonded to Maurice, who was Matilda's mate, but Hamlet and Clotilda were not partnered. None of them quite understood how that all worked, but thought that time would answer those questions.

Hamlet was over six feet tall, with greying hair and kind blue eyes that twinkled as the students wandered in sluggishly, reluctantly, and slowly. The classroom was large enough for twenty desks and had a huge blackboard up at the front behind Hamlet's desk. There were windows all along one side that looked out onto the central courtyard at Havenshold.

"You're probably wondering why you are here," began Hamlet. The students all nodded. "There's a lot to learn about being a dragon rider. You need to learn Draconia's history from the *very* beginning. You need to learn about government and how the country functions. You need to learn math and science—especially aerodynamics—so that when you and your dragon begin flying, you'll understand about wind currents, updrafts, and other things. You need to be able to write well, as you'll be communicating with all parts of the land on the King's behalf. You need to learn about the other three nations so that you understand the dynamics between the countries, and know how to stop trouble before it starts. You'll need to learn the care of the other magical creatures—the dolphins, the gryphons, and the unicorns—just as all their riders learn dragon care, because none of us know when or where we might need help, or need to assist others. And then, there are a myriad of smaller topics to learn as well—meteorology, leather working, metal working, and so on."

Hamlet smiled. "The next nine years of your life, until you're finished with your apprenticeship, will be *very* busy. You'll spend your mornings in classes and your afternoons in training—sometimes with your dragon and sometimes without."

Emily looked at Anne and they rolled their eyes rolled. *Gads,* thought Emily. *I had no idea that being a dragon rider required such rigorous training. Why did my brothers never say anything?* She looked over at Joseph, who appeared to be bored and unimpressed by this. She glanced at William, and noticed that he appeared riveted by every word Hamlet uttered. *Makes sense,* she thought, remembering how they'd been in regular school.

"OK," said Hamlet. "Let's pass out the books and get started."

So her new life began.

Emily learned a lot that she never thought she would have to learn. Then she had to teach it to Esmeralda. Hamlet said that it was a dragon rider's responsibility—to be sure his or her dragon was as well educated as its rider, because dragons could communicate with humans, the dragon needed to know as much or more than the rider. Hamlet also said that teaching someone else was the fastest and most effective way to learn something yourself. Emily found out very quickly just how true that was.

Emily enjoyed teaching Esmeralda as Esmeralda was very bright. When Esmeralda asked questions Emily couldn't answer, Emily had to go back to class to find the answer herself. *It really is a very effective way to educate both dragon and rider,* thought Emily.

The years flew by. Emily was allowed to go home for one Sunday afternoon a month, but otherwise she was at Havenshold, training. It was hard. Emily learned hand-to-hand combat, self-defense, first aid for both rider and dragon, as well as advanced math and science. She learned the complicated dragon rider culture where dragons mated for life, but that didn't mean their riders did, and the riders could have families of their own, making for a complex, but rich, community.

By the time she was eighteen, she and Esmeralda had learned enough to begin their flying lessons together. Esmeralda had been flying with the other dragons for several years now, strengthening her wings and body, learning about air currents and so forth, but it was very different to have a rider on her back.

Emily remembered the first time she flew on Esmeralda. Esmeralda was so tall now that Emily had to climb up on one of Esmeralda's bent knees and reach for a spine to lift herself up. The first time was so awkward she wasn't sure she would ever get up, but Esmeralda had learned how to sit and position herself to help Emily.

Some riders, like Joseph, preferred to walk up their dragon's tails. Joseph—stocky with short jet black hair—had never been particularly athletic. He spent his days with his nose in a book before becoming a rider, and even now, he chose the least athletic way of mounting.

Both Emily and Anne had trained in gymnastics, and so they soon developed the dragon rider's vault and were quick to mount after a few false starts. William had grown very tall—at least six and a half feet—and was no longer a bumbling kid. He found it easy to take a running leap, bounce off Thunder's knee, and land on Thunder's back.

It was interesting, Emily thought, *that the four friends were so close and yet so different. The way they mounted their dragons reflected a lot about them as individuals.*

Their first ride had been absolutely incredible. Emily and Esmeralda took off from the landing field with Emily gripping the harness as tightly as possible. Esmeralda wobbled just a bit, as she wasn't used to the extra weight on her back. Once in the air, they soared through the sky, and it felt as if they were the only beings anywhere. Emily quickly realized that Esmeralda would never let her fall, and so she relaxed, which made Esmeralda relax. All too soon, the half hour allotted for their first flight was over and they landed back on the field. They both knew that they would be in the air whenever they could.

The best part of the day for both Emily and Esmeralda became the flying lessons. It was fun to have them with their friends. Emily was amazed when she realized how much they all had grown. William was no longer a shy, scared, little boy. He had gained confidence as his abilities and his talents grew. He and Thunder were a very strong pair. As brown dragons were the most sensitive to weather changes, William and Thunder were preparing for a career in climatology. In addition, they were developing an unexpected gift for telepathic communications with others.

Anne and Samantha were also excelling in the yellow dragon's strongest field—telepathy—and they would soon be learning how to pick up thoughts of people and animals far below them as they flew over the land—they were to be able to spot difficulties before they got out of hand.

Joseph and his green dragon, Spruce, were quickly becoming the fastest team among the new riders, which was just what they ought to do. Greens were messengers—dependable, speedy, and with long memories.

Finally, Emily and Esmeralda were becoming the leaders of the group. Dragon riders had always had a female purple dragon as their leader, and Emily and Esmeralda were falling into that role naturally. Female purple dragons were even rarer than males, and Matilda was the only other one on the active duty list.

The group spent the next three years learning their assigned tasks. They flew on missions with older dragon riders from time to time. As they approached their twentieth-first birthdays, they were given more responsibilities, and more free time to explore the kingdom with their dragons.

Emily was very happy one day when she and Esmeralda were out on their own and came across Gregory. He was on horseback checking out something on his father's land. Esmeralda and Emily landed at a distance so they didn't spook Gregory's horse, then waited for Gregory to approach. Emily was glad for the chance to talk with him. She hadn't seen much of him since the hatching many years before.

"Hi, Gregory," she called with a wave.

"Emily! It's great to see you," answered Gregory. "Your dragon is magnificent."

"Let me introduce you to her," said Emily. "Her name is Esmeralda. Esmeralda, this is Gregory."

Esmeralda spoke to Gregory in his mind. *Pleased to meet you, Gregory.* Gregory's eyes popped open wide, and he smiled broadly.

"How are you doing?" asked Emily.

"I'm doing well enough," answered Gregory. "But I have to admit, my father's being difficult. He still feels I should have been chosen as a dragon rider all those years ago, but it's because he has visions of being on the throne himself. If he can't, then I'm the next best thing. He never has gotten over the fact that *he* wasn't chosen. Now he's pushing me to take over some of the responsibilities for running his land."

"Parents sometimes try to live their dreams through their children, I guess," said Emily with a shrug. Esmeralda's warmth at her side was a reassuring constant.

"Yeah, but you know, as amazing as dragon riders are, I never *wanted* to be a dragon rider. I don't even want to be a baron. I want to be a volcanologist, but my father won't hear of it." A smile spread over his face and he leaned in as if she were a conspirator. "I'm studying secretly."

"Well, I know you can do it and I know you'll find a way to make your dreams come true. I'll be pulling for you," said Emily with a huge smile. "It was great running into you, but we've got to get back to Havenshold."

"Yeah, and I have to keep hunting for lost sheep. See you later," replied Gregory. He stepped back and watched as Esmeralda bent her front left leg, and Emily vaulted from the leg onto Esmeralda's back. Esmeralda heard him think, *She makes it look so easy and natural.*

Emily and Esmeralda lifted off the ground smoothly and easily. Gregory smiled as he saw Emily and Esmeralda soar high above him, dipping a wing to wave at him, before they turned for Havenshold.

— 5 —

Graduation Day

Graduation day had finally arrived. By the end of the day, Emily's apprenticeship would be over and she would be a junior dragon rider. She would be done with classes, done with boring drills, and done with the teasing by the full-fledged dragon riders. Her career would be starting.

Emily dressed quickly and headed out to do her morning chores. She and Esmeralda had a lot to accomplish before the ceremonies at noon. Best of all, she would be able to see her family as the entire population of Draconia would be here.

Esmeralda thought, *You sure love to exaggerate!*

OK, thought Emily, *You're right, but I bet everyone from Havenshold will be here!*

Esmeralda slyly stuck her thoughts in. *Including Gregory Geldsmith!*

Emily blushed, grateful that their telepathic communication couldn't be overheard.

But they were too busy now to think about any of that. The grounds had to be in tip-top shape. This was a task given to the oldest apprentices—in her nearly nine years here, there had been two more hatchings, meaning there were two younger classes of apprentices. Soon there would be a third hatching on the next winter solstice, only a few months after graduation to be held on the fall equinox.

The senior apprentices had to work hard. Emily ran into Anne, Joseph, and William at various times in the morning, each looking just as harried as she was.

Joseph called out, "Wouldn't you think on *our* day they'd cut us some slack?"

"Not a chance," Emily called back. "They wouldn't want us to feel *too* important after all." She laughed. "We may be senior now, but soon we'll be at the bottom again as the newest dragon riders."

Finally, it was time to get cleaned up. Emily and Esmeralda took a good soak in the hot springs. Esmeralda said, *Sure is nice to live atop a volcano!*

Emily had to agree. *Yeah, as long as it's a tamed one.*

Esmeralda chortled. Even after nearly nine years, Emily was still amazed at how wonderful it was to be able to talk to someone in her head all the time, even when they weren't next to each other. Their telepathy held over a distance of several miles, and she knew the older dragon riders could communicate over even greater distances. It felt incredible to be so close to another being. Emily treasured that feeling as she and Esmeralda prepared for the ceremony.

Emily made sure that Esmeralda had plenty of oil on her so that her iridescent purple wings would shine in the sun when they performed their graduation dance in the sky. Then they headed out to wait with the other twelve senior apprentices for the ceremony.

She knew that not only were her dragon rider brothers—Jake and Hans—there, but so were her parents and her younger brothers and sister. There was a special observation box for the families. For today, Jake and Hans would be *there* cheering her on, instead of with their dragons on patrol—or doing whatever it was that real dragon riders did.

Suddenly, Emily felt scared. She had no real idea what it was like to be a dragon rider. Yes, she had come in at the top of her class, but what did she really *know* about being a dragon rider.

Esmeralda said in her head, *We may be new, but we know a lot, and we'll figure out whatever we need to in order to do our jobs well, whatever those jobs are. We'll be determining our own path based on our strengths. We'll figure it out!*

Emily thought back to her, *With you, I can do anything.*

The senior apprentices and their dragons were escorted into the arena by the dragon riders who had graduated three years ago. They were joking, saying, "Now we won't be the lowest newest riders anymore. It's your turn to get all the dirty jobs!"

The apprentices groaned as they remembered what it had been like to be the newest apprentices, and how much they had enjoyed it when younger apprentices joined the ranks.

Clotilda, with Matilda at her side, congratulated each dragon rider and presented them with a beautiful, hand-woven scarf made in the color of their dragon. Each dragon was given a gold chain with a stone that matched their color. Then came the moment Emily had been both anticipating and dreading. Each dragon and rider had to choreograph an aerial dance and then perform it. As was her right as a purple dragon rider, Emily would be the last to perform, which meant she had to be at least as good—if not *better*—than all the others. The audience would have seen twelve gorgeous dances before hers.

Anne's dance was as lovely as Anne herself. Emily applauded with everyone else when it was done. She was very pleased to see William manage his dance with confidence and without any apparent nerves at all. It was hard to remember back to the scared little boy she had known nine years ago. Joseph, cocky as always, brought his dance off without a single hitch. Both boys—*Men,* she realized, *they're boys no longer*—had opted for very athletic dances, whereas Anne had opted for an aerial ballet that was smooth and flowing. The other dances were also wonderful. Emily was very nervous, but at the same time strangely confident, when it was finally her turn.

The dances only lasted three minutes each, but they seemed a lifetime. The dragon and rider had to demonstrate unity—a bond that was unbreakable.

When it was finally their time, Emily and Esmeralda flew into the air and performed a dance which was both athletic and graceful. They soared above the crowds in the cool autumn air. Emily had a rainbow of scarves which she twirled as Esmeralda twisted this way and that. The two of them were in perfect harmony and soon forgot that anyone was watching. They just enjoyed their movements, flowing from one to another without any hesitations. When they were done, the applause was deafening. Esmeralda gloated, *I knew we could wow them!* But Emily just smiled and thought back, *I love you! You are so special.*

After the ceremonies, the newly graduated riders were permitted to meet with their family and friends. When Emily was allowed her Sunday afternoons at home, she had to go without Esmeralda. Now, the two of them stood proudly in the line of new riders and their dragons to receive congratulations and hugs. It was *marvelous* to be able to show Esmeralda off!

Emily's younger brothers, Robert and Michael, were in awe. They wanted to pet Esmeralda. Robert was now sixteen and studying to be an architect, and Michael, at fourteen, wasn't sure, but thought he wanted to be either a geologist or a biologist. And then there was Hannah, who was just twelve, and who hoped to be a candidate at the next hatching in three months. She had watched the ceremonies, absolutely spell-bound, and

Emily was sure she was wondering if one day the family would be gathered around her the way they now were around Emily.

Hannah, with red cheeks and downcast eyes, asked, "Is it all right if I pet you, Esmeralda?" Emily was impressed. Neither Robert nor Michael had bothered to ask. They'd taken it as their right, but neither had showed any interest in being a dragon rider, either. They didn't really understand—as was unfortunately true of much of Draconia's population—what *magical* creatures dragons truly were. But Hannah knew and she treated Esmeralda with respect.

Hannah jumped. Esmeralda hadn't answered aloud as Hannah had expected. Dragons *can* use human speech if they have to, but Esmeralda chose to honor Hannah by speaking with her telepathically, something Esmeralda could only do with certain people—usually other riders, but sometimes very sensitive people.

Esmeralda said telepathically, *I would be honored to have you touch me, young Hannah.*

Later, Emily thanked Esmeralda. "You know that was the very best present you could have given Hannah!"

"I know," said Esmeralda. "I'm confident that Hannah will be picked as a candidate for the next hatching. She *feels* like a rider, but don't tell her that! She needs to have the full experience, just as you did."

Emily laughed. Esmeralda was wise and wonderful.

After all the congratulations, the day was turned over to games, food, and fireworks that evening. Emily and Esmeralda stayed with Emily's family and had a wonderful day. At one point, Gregory stopped by to congratulate Emily and Esmeralda. Emily blushed when he said he thought her dance was the best. As he talked, he kept looking over his shoulder apprehensively.

Emily finally asked him if he were OK. He said, "I'm worried about my father. He's acting strangely. I know he's hugely disappointed that I wasn't chosen, and I know he's only here because of his standing in the community, but nevertheless, he's being more than just grumpy. I saw him talking with some very disreputable guys—a couple of thugs. I've never seen him mix with *that* sort before."

"Do you think he's up to something?" asked Emily.

"I don't know," answered Gregory. "But everyone who's anyone in Draconia is here today—including King Jacob and his family—and my father's so obsessed with power that I *cringe* to think what he could be plotting."

"We could have a look around if that would help," said Emily. Her eyebrows shot up. "Hey, I've got an idea. You see how some of the other new dragon riders are giving rides to friends and family? How would you like a ride on Esmeralda? We could observe without it being obvious. If Esmeralda's willing, we could also take Hannah, so it would look just like all the other rides. What do you think?"

Gregory looked at Esmeralda. He was startled when he heard Esmeralda in his head saying, *Why thank you, kind sir!* This was followed by what could only be described as a dragon smile, as she fluttered her long eyelashes at him.

Emily asked Esmeralda—telepathically so that Esmeralda could answer honestly—if she were willing to have a couple of passengers, and Esmeralda agreed. Emily then asked Hannah, who agreed instantly. Emily had Esmeralda bend her front left leg and then showed Gregory how to climb up. Next she gave Hannah a boost as Gregory reached for Hannah's hand and swung her up easily. Finally, Emily vaulted up onto Esmeralda's back. Soon, Emily, Gregory, and Hannah were airborne on Esmeralda—Hannah sandwiched between the two adults—and they slowly circled the arena and all the people.

They spotted King Jacob and his family, including his son Rupert, heir to the throne.

Next they spotted Baron Geldsmith—Gregory's father. Emily realized that Gregory was right. The Baron was off in a secluded area behind the food booths with two very unsavory looking people. The Baron quickly broke off the discussion and headed over to a group of other nobles while the thugs headed into the crowds and disappeared.

Esmeralda landed and Emily helped Gregory and Hannah down. Hannah was so excited by the ride, she kept hugging and kissing Esmeralda. Esmeralda would have blushed if dragons could. Emily thought, *Esmeralda, you're right. If she gets chosen she will be a natural.*

Gregory was worried. He said, "I didn't want to spoil your special day, but I'm glad you saw what I saw."

Emily said, "Don't be silly. My day has been wonderful. Besides, I'm a dragon rider now—not an apprentice—and looking out for trouble is what we do."

Gregory smiled. "Well, just know that whatever my father does, I'm on the side of the dragon riders. You can count on me. Now, shall we sample some of the wonderful food?" Gregory took Hannah by one hand and Emily by the other, and with Esmeralda leading the way, they headed to the food booths to stock up and then join Emily's family to enjoy the evening's entertainment.

— 6 —

Baron's Ultimatum

A week later, the summoning bell rang at Havenshold, waking all the riders before dawn. The bell was only rung at times of crisis or emergencies, so all dragon riders hurried to the main hall to learn what was wrong.

As soon as all the riders were present, Clotilda called for silence. She then announced that King Jacob had summoned all dragon riders to the Palace in the Capitol city of Draconia. She said that the dragon riders had to appear *without* their dragons, something that caused an uproar.

Clotilda said, "I know, this is *very* unusual, and normally I wouldn't agree to leaving Matilda behind, nor would Matilda agree to my going without her, but the King sent me a private coded message inside the public summons. He indicated that he really has no choice in this, that he's being coerced, and that the situation is both unusual and very dangerous. He could give me no details, but I feel we *owe* it to King Jacob to follow his wishes. He's a very good King, and he too was once a dragon rider, so he knows what he is asking of us."

There was still a lot of muttering, but the riders soon realized that there was no choice. It would be a long, hard day's travel for the riders to make their way to the castle without their dragons. They would be hiking, since dragon riders did not keep many horses—horses and dragons usually didn't mix very well. It was a very cold fall. Clotilda insisted that only about a quarter of the riders would go. She had no intention of taking all riders and leaving the new eggs unprotected, and she didn't want the dragons left *alone.* This summons smelled of a plot.

Clotilda selected a contingent of fifty dragon riders to head to the Capitol. She didn't want to appear to be breaking the summons, but only the dragon riders knew exactly how many riders and dragons there were. Even at large public events, such as last week's graduation, Clotilda made sure that only a token number of riders were visible. The dragon riders had a history of being made unwelcome on previous worlds where they had been forced out time and again. Clotilda didn't want anyone to realize how many riders there were in case people got fearful.

The dragons and riders had lived here for five hundred years, having dream-travelled from another solar system. Clotilda wanted them to be able to stay. However, no matter how much the dragons and their riders did for the nations of this world, there was still the underlying fear that they could be turned against at any moment by those who did not understand dragons or magical bonding. She knew that the other lands took similar precautions with their magical creatures and riders.

Clotilda selected riders from all levels and colors, even though the dragons wouldn't be going. Emily, Anne, Joseph, and William were the riders chosen from their graduating class, so they, along with the other selected riders, quickly gathered their gear and headed out. It would be a very long, cold hike. The Capitol was over twenty-five miles from Havenshold. That meant journeying through a lot of mountainous terrain. Riders grumbled along the way. Emily frequently heard someone or another say, "I sure wish we were flying. It would be so much easier and faster."

Emily was able to communicate with Esmeralda for the first five or ten miles, and that was very comforting, but after that, she couldn't reach Esmeralda's mind. Emily knew that Clotilda was in constant contact with Matilda, and that their link was so strong that they would be in contact even in the Capitol. They'd been bonded for nearly forty years, and Matilda was a purple dragon. The purples were the strongest in telepathy, followed closely by yellows.

Finally, tired and cold, the dragon riders marched into the Capitol. They found themselves immediately flanked by the Palace guard and escorted—rather rudely—to the Palace where they were forced to turn over all their weapons. That had never happened before and added to their unease. They were not allowed to wash or eat, but instead were herded into the King's conference hall where all the barons and nobles were congregating. Apparently, everyone knew just when they would arrive.

King Jacob greeted Clotilda and thanked her for coming. Introductions were quickly interrupted by Baron Geldsmith, who proved to be the person controlling the meeting.

Emily thought, *Clotilda was right to be worried!* She turned to look at her friends with wide eyes.

Baron Geldsmith—a large burly man whose grey hair was thinning noticeably—started right in, ranting and raving. "We've put up with dragons for much too long. I have evidence that the dragons have been *attacking* my sheep and my cattle. My herds have been nearly destroyed. We can*not* allow such savage animals to live in our midst any longer. The dragons must all be destroyed."

The dragon riders glanced at Clotilda, each one looking as stricken as Emily felt. Clotilda looked to King Jacob for permission to speak. After his nod, she said, "What evidence do you have, Baron, that it was dragons who were responsible? I assure you—"

Baron Geldsmith interrupted and said, "I don't care what you say or what your *assurances* are. I know my sheep and cattle are gone, and I know it was *dragons who took them.* My manager saw them attacking our flocks. And what was worse is that the dragons had *dragon riders* on them when they attacked."

Clotilda was not allowed to reply, but every rider there knew that these accusations were in no way true. In the first place, no dragon would attack livestock. Why should they? Havenshold raised all the food the dragons and riders needed, and then some. It was self-contained and self-sufficient. Clotilda appeared to be staring off into space, but Emily and the other riders knew that she was in contact with Matilda, who in turn was letting those in Havenshold know what was going on.

Baron Geldsmith asked the other barons and nobles if they had suffered similar losses. A few of the Baron's closest friends said yes. The others, although silent, were clearly under the Baron's control—they all had downcast eyes. Baron Geldsmith asked King Jacob, "Well? Will you order the execution of all dragons now that you know what *atrocities* they are committing?"

Emily noticed that King Jacob looked very old, tired, and drawn. He looked nothing like the happy man he'd been at her graduation only a week earlier, enjoying the festivities with his family.

King Jacob thought for a long moment before he spoke. "We only have one eye witness account, Baron, to support your accusations. But, if what you say is true, then it is a *very* serious matter."

"Are you doubting my word?" asked Baron Geldsmith, moving aggressively toward the King. "May I remind you that you *wouldn't be King* without the support of the barons and nobles, and *I* am their leader. I *insist* on justice!"

King Jacob replied, "I have every intention of giving justice, but I won't order a wholesale genocide because of *one* account." The Baron started to interrupt again, but King Jacob held up his hand and called for silence. "What I will order is that *all* dragons, and their riders, be confined to Havenshold. There will be no patrols and no visits to other nations. Clotilda, you will lock the entrances to Havenshold and require that all your dragons and riders to stay inside. Is that clear?"

Clotilda looked deep into King Jacob's eyes. His pain and conflict were clear. She agreed to his order. "Dragons and dragon riders have always been *yours* to command, your majesty. You know that to be true. We will obey your orders."

King Jacob looked very relieved, though still sad. "Thank you, Clotilda. I know I can count on you. I *will* get to the bottom of this, I promise you, and I will keep you apprised by my personal messengers of any developments. Rest assured that as long as you remain within the confines of Havenshold, you and yours will have my personal guarantee of safety."

"That may be true," snarled Baron Geldsmith, "but any riders or dragons found *outside* of Havenshold will be *killed on sight,* no questions asked. I have men who will carry out those instructions to the letter."

Clotilda looked at the Baron and replied very coldly. "We are not *intimidated* or *frightened* by your *threats.* King Jacob knows that we will do whatever he commands, and whatever you may think, we have a very high sense of honor. You would be well advised to *remember* that."

"Don't you *dare* speak to me that way!" roared the Baron.

Clotilda turned to King Jacob and said, "Your majesty, do we have your leave to depart?"

King Jacob nodded and flexed his hand, as if his fingers hurt. Clotilda turned to her dragon riders and motioned them to follow her. Once they were outside the meeting room, she demanded the return of their weapons. Weapons returned, the dragon riders marched smartly out of the Capitol. They marched about five miles away from the city toward Havenshold before Clotilda called a halt. "We need to rest and eat, but after, we need to march as quickly as possible back to Havenshold."

Joseph could contain himself no longer. "We aren't going to let the Baron get away with this, are we?"

"Yeah," said someone else. "We didn't do *anything* wrong! And not only Draconia, but this entire *world* looks to us for protection and energy. If we didn't monitor the volcano and siphon off its enormous energies, this whole world could be destroyed by a single eruption."

Clotilda called for order. "King Jacob knows that very well. Remember, he was once a dragon rider himself, until the death of his beloved Henrietta. I saw *something* in his eyes, which leads me to believe that there's enormous pressure being put on him. It will be up to us to find out what Baron Geldsmith is up to and to stop him at all costs."

Emily asked, "How can we do that if we follow the King's orders, as you said we would?"

Clotilda smiled. "I've known King Jacob for many years. He was my mentor when I was an apprentice. We developed hand signals so we could communicate in dangerous situations. During the meeting, he signaled me that he needed help. My promise to him, which we will honor, is to guard the King and the kingdom. We will do *whatever* it takes. We all know that Baron Geldsmith made up the story about his sheep and cattle. When you are a deceiving, evil person, it never occurs to you that others take the matter of honor and truth seriously. The Baron is in for some big surprises."

The riders felt a lot better after hearing Clotilda's words.

"But now we need to march as quickly as we can. Rest time is over. Let's head out and get home."

Without a thought about how far it was, or how tired they were, the riders picked up the pace. It would not take them as long to get home as it had for them to reach the Capitol.

As they got closer and closer to Havenshold, each rider began picking up the thoughts of their dragons, which helped them maintain strength and endurance. At last, Havenshold was in sight and they broke individually into runs to get inside.

It was time for plans to be made.

— 7 —

Dragon Riders Scheme

Emily woke up the morning after her return to Havenshold, remembering the rigors of hiking fifty miles in one day. She'd collapsed late last night after their return, falling asleep next to Esmeralda in her nest. Not only had the trip been hard, but it had been the first time since the hatching that she had been unable to communicate with Esmeralda. Emily worried about the Baron's ultimatum concerning the dragons. Clotilda had called a meeting for this morning right after breakfast for all the riders and dragons who were currently in Havenshold. Emily and Esmeralda got ready quickly and headed out to the arena.

When Emily arrived, she found a spot next to Anne, Joseph, and William. The air smelled crisp and clean. It was lovely to look down on the dragon eggs incubating in the hot sands. Several riders were in the sand turning the eggs, but everyone else—including the dragons—lined the top of the stone wall surrounding the arena. When everyone was gathered, Clotilda called the meeting to order. "I think everyone now knows what happened when we were in the Capitol. First, are there any questions?" Clotilda asked.

"What about the dragons and riders who *aren't* here?" yelled one rider.

"That's a very good question. King Jacob forced the Baron into allowing a forty-eight-hour truce, which begins today. Thankfully, we were allowed time to regain Havenshold and inform you all of the proceedings *before* the forty-eight-hour countdown began. I told the Baron it would take longer to get here than it did, but we need every minute we can find."

Clotilda looked around at her beloved dragons and riders before proceeding. "I know that there has to be something extremely serious going on here. When King Jacob lost his Henrietta in a terrible storm, he nearly died himself. It took him *years* to recover. The fact that he had been a dragon rider led to his becoming King when the last King died without an heir. As I hope you all know by now, the provisions for Draconia were set up so that a dragon rider, or direct heir of a dragon rider, would *always* be King. We have been turned on in too many other worlds, forced out, *feared,* because we are different. So when we arrived in this world—a wonderful world with other magical creatures and riders—we followed their examples and set up a government to protect us, as well as all of our citizens who may no longer be dragon riders."

Emily's brother, Hans, called out, "Then why is King Jacob *allowing* this? Why is he not *protecting* us?" Emily noticed that Hans looked very unkempt—unshaven with his brown hair sticking up in the back.

"That," said Clotilda, "is a *very good* question. Only a crisis of the deepest severity would cause Jacob to give even an *inch* to Baron Geldsmith—someone he has loathed for years. I saw the pain in King Jacob's eyes. I know he's being forced into this. I can't imagine what hold the Baron has over him."

All of a sudden there was an uproar at the entrance to the arena and Gregory came bursting in. He was surrounded by dragon riders who tried to stop him. "Please!" he shouted. "Let me speak. I have information!"

Clotilda motioned to the dragon riders to let go of Gregory. "We'll hear what you have to say, but you must convince us that you are not here to spy for your father."

Gregory—a tall, ruggedly handsome man with light brown hair and piercing green eyes—burst out. "My father is trying to take over the throne of Draconia and maybe even our entire world!"

Clotilda responded, "I knew he was greedy, but had no idea he was that greedy."

Gregory nodded. "My father raised both Lance and me to be strong and ruthless. He beat us if we showed kindness. I tried to please him, because I knew of his pain...but I knew I could never be *like* him. My father was devastated as a boy when he wasn't selected as a candidate for the dragon hatchings, but after he married my mother and I was born, he seemed content to build the largest baronial holding in the country and become head of the nobles—which he's done. At first, he was a fair leader and he got followers by helping them and taking care of them, but that was only while my mother was alive. Once she died, he became ruthless. He's been blackmailing all the other nobles to gain control over them. He knows their secrets and exploits his knowledge. That's why none of the other nobles spoke up against him at the hearing."

Clotilda said, "Well, that makes things much clearer. You're saying that not all the nobles are truly behind him? How do you know this?"

"From a very young age," said Gregory, "I enjoyed exploring our castle. I discovered lots of dusty passages that I suspect had long been forgotten. There's one that leads to a small window that overlooks my father's private chambers where he meets with his *supposed* allies. I used to eavesdrop, thinking I would learn what my father wanted from me and how I should act. However, as I grew and learned more about people, I was absolutely horrified by the way my father manipulated those around him. I could even see him doing it with Lance, encouraging him to be ruthless. Lance is now a bully and is *hated* by his peers. My father has always said that I am too soft—just like my mother." Gregory straightened. "He could not have given me higher praise."

Clotilda nodded. "This is good information, but how can it help us now? If your father has strangleholds on the other nobles, they are hardly going to come over to our side. And your brother is now of an age to be carrying weapons and fighting as well, helping your father in his evil plot. Thank heavens Lance was not picked as a candidate for the egg hatching when he was younger. I've always wondered how the dragons pick candidates, and how they can see so deeply and accurately into the hearts of young people to know what kind of people they will grow into, but I'm so very grateful that they *can*."

Gregory said, "I've wondered about that too. When I was twelve, I kept saying to myself, *don't pick me!* Even at that age, I knew I didn't want to be a dragon rider. I *love* the dragons," he quickly continued, as he looked up at all the magnificent creatures surrounding the arena. "I think they are absolutely the most fantastic beings in existence, and I would be honored by their friendship, but I want to be a scientist, a volcanologist, and I want to be able to help you—dragons and dragon riders alike—without your responsibilities. I was very relieved when I wasn't chosen, but my father was furious. I was way for him to gain power. He's never seen me as a real person. He even made me say I *wanted* a second chance. Three years later, I was chosen as a candidate for the second time...I think the dragons, in their wisdom, knew that for the peace of the land I had to be picked as a candidate, even though *they* knew I'd never be chosen by a newly hatched dragon."

Clotilda was thoughtful for a minute. "What you say rings true. Matilda remembers things just as you have related them, and your thoughts on the dragons' reasons are right. You weren't picked as a candidate, because you didn't *want* to be. Dragons never force anyone. You were picked the second time—and Matilda apologizes for the anxiety that caused you—for political reasons. She knew no dragon would force themselves on you."

"My father was also furious," Gregory continued, "to find out that Lance's age would keep him from ever being selected as a candidate. He was either too young or too old. He kept hoping an exception would be made, but it wasn't. Finally, my father has realized that the only way he could gain the power he so *desperately* craved wasn't by using the dragon riders as he had hoped, but by *eliminating* them...and that's what his current path is trying to accomplish. We *must* stop him." The desperation on Gregory's face was evident.

Clotilda looked deep into Gregory's eyes and said, "You are standing against your father in this? That is not an easy thing to do. *You* are his *heir.*"

Gregory stood up straight and tall, planted his feet firmly as his jaw tightened, and proclaimed, "I may be my father's eldest, but I'll *never* be his heir. I'm my mother's son and I'll not be a party to his treachery. My mother loved all creatures... she thought the dragons were incredible beings. She would never condone what my father is doing and neither will I. My father is lying about dragons attacking herds. He's so warped that he doesn't understand those with values and honor. His gamekeeper, Henry, is just as bad. The two of them are working together. I know that Henry is as deeply involved as my father."

Emily remembered graduation day. She shouted from the back of the crowd, "Gregory, what about those men we saw your father with on graduation day?" Immediately her head drooped as she worried that she had spoken out of turn.

Clotilda looked at Emily, beckoned her forward, and smiled. "OK," Clotilda said. "Suppose you two tell us about that."

Emily looked at Gregory, who nodded. She continued, "After the ceremony, when I was chatting with my family, Gregory came over to congratulate me. He looked very worried and he confessed that he'd seen his father talking to a couple really unsavory looking men. I suggested that Esmeralda and I take him—and my sister Hannah—for a ride the way others were doing as part of the celebrations. Esmeralda was happy to do it. She even spoke to Gregory telepathically."

"Really?" said Clotilda. "That's impressive, but please continue."

Gregory picked up the story. "We circled above the crowd and spotted my father with the two thugs. To be honest, as I think back on that moment, I'm not even sure they were from Draconia. They had the look of fishermen, but very nasty looking ones. My father finished talking with them and they took off into the crowds. We couldn't follow. My father headed over to a group of nobles and started talking to them. What seemed strange was, all the time my father was talking to the thugs, he kept looking in the direction of King Jacob and his family. Both Emily and I had commented on how happy the King looked celebrating with his family, so we noticed when my father was also watching them."

"That gives us lots to work on," answered Clotilda. "Thank you, Gregory. We are very lucky to have you on our side. If ever we can do anything for you, just let us know. Meanwhile, we need to try to track these thugs and discover what the baron is plotting. Let's break for lunch and reconvene this afternoon."

Everyone headed out to the dining hall.

Emily caught up with Gregory. "I'm so glad you came," she said.

He looked down at his boots and said, "I couldn't stand by and watch my father try to kill Esmeralda and all the other dragons."

— 8 —

Counteroffensive

After lunch, the riders and dragons reconvened. Emily watched as Clotilda entered, marveling at her quiet dignity. Clotilda was one of the tallest dragon riders—well over six feet with short, neatly cropped, grey hair and blue eyes behind her octagonal wire-framed glasses. Her face was weathered from being outside most of her life, but there was no hardness about her. She cared for all the people in Havenshold, whether dragon rider or not. She had been in command of Havenshold for nearly twenty years and she carried her command with dignity and honor.

Once everyone was present Clotilda said, "The picture is forming that Baron Geldsmith has a *strong* hold over King Jacob, and from what Emily and Gregory observed at the graduation ceremonies, I would say that the hold involves King Jacob's *family* in some way."

The riders nodded in agreement. Clotilda continued. "Our first responsibility must be to notify all dragons and riders who are currently away from Havenshold on missions or leave. About one-third of our dragons and riders need to be contacted quickly and told either to stay where they are—in the case of dragons and riders serving as ambassadors to the other three nations—or get back here within the prescribed forty-eight hours. Are there any suggestions for this?"

William quietly, but confidently, said, "I've been studying the telepathic nature of dragon and rider communication. Thunder and I have managed to contact almost all the other dragons and riders telepathically."

There was a burst of applause for such a wonderful accomplishment by such a new dragon rider.

William continued, "Our range isn't the best, but I think Thunder and I can reach *most* of the dragons who are within Draconia, especially if we fly out about fifty miles. I think that once we've started contacting them, the other dragons will be able to continue the pattern. I know not all dragons like talking with anyone except their own rider, but I believe in this emergency they'll see the benefits and try."

Clotilda said, "I knew you and Thunder were up to something with your research, but how wonderful to find out just how successful you've been. I've always thought it was dreadful that, in some ways, we dragon riders have become just as narrow and insular as the general populace. We spend time with only dragons of the same color...*You* are an inspiration to us all, William and Thunder. From here on out, I will encourage all dragons and riders to do the same. First, Emily and Esmeralda are communicating with non-riders, and now you are improving our telepathic skills! Well done to *both* of you!"

There was a gentle applause from the other riders. Many of the older riders were nodding in appreciation. Emily realized that Clotilda led by example and encouragement and that was what made her such a good leader. *Will I ever be able to do that?* she thought.

"OK," continued Clotilda. "Let's set up a plan. William and Thunder will head out to contact as many dragons and riders as they can. However, William, I don't want you going out alone.

You are inexperienced and the Baron has shown himself to be ruthless. Is there anyone you would want to help you?"

William nodded. "Jake and Harmony have been helping us. They are our mentors, so if they could come, I think it would be a big help. Harmony has a very long range for telepathic communication. She's touched nearly as many as Thunder and I have."

"So be it," said Clotilda. "William, Jake, head out as soon as you can, and let's see how many of our dragons and riders we can get back here. But under *no* circumstances are you to engage in fighting with the Baron's men. You *absolutely* must be back here before the time limit expires, say within forty-four hours. I don't want any arrow happy barons starting their attack early."

William nodded. Jake said, "Harmony and I will take care of him, Clotida, I promise. Not only are William and Thunder on a wonderful research track, but they are also among my sister's best friends. She'd never speak to me again if I let anything happen to them." Jake smiled up at Emily and waved as he and William headed out to gather their gear.

"William and Jake will be covering Draconia, but what about our ambassadors in the other three lands?" asked Clotilda.

Hans, not to be outdone, said, "Fire Dancer and I could fly along Draconia's borders and contact all the ambassadors. What should we ask them to do? Stay put or return home?"

Clotilda thanked Hans and said, "I think, given that we really don't know the extent of the Baron's treachery, we should ask them to stay put and keep listening for any information. We can trust our riders not to divulge the threat here unless they feel confident that they will gain supporters for our side."

Hans agreed. He and Fire Dancer headed out as well, promising to be back within the forty-four hour cutoff.

"What next?" asked Clotilda. "Does anyone else have any suggestions?"

Gregory said, "I think I should return home and see what else I can learn. Now that I have an idea of what my father is up to, I can spy more effectively on him and Henry."

Clotilda said, "We appreciate that, but *be careful.* Your father must know that you don't agree with him. We don't want to see anything happen to you either, dragon friend. I think we will send Emily and Esmeralda out after dark to patrol your father's lands. He won't think it too threatening to see them, because he knows you are friends. She is also young enough that he might think she is just restless and disobedient. If you are in trouble, find a way to let Emily and Esmeralda know. They will get you out of there."

"Thanks." Gregory smiled and nodded at Clotilda.

Clotilda continued, "But please stay here until the end of our meeting so that you hear everything.

"One thing that bothers me is that both Emily and Gregory thought that the thugs the Baron is using looked like *fishermen,*" said Clotilda. "The Baron's land is right on the border with Sanwight. Would anyone like to see if they can discover anything amiss in Sanwight? I know Hans will be back with his reports from our ambassadors there, but I don't want to miss an opportunity, and we can only move freely for *now*—" she paused as she looked at her watch, "—another forty-six hours."

Anne and Joseph started talking at the same time. They looked at each other, and then Anne continued. "Joseph and I have been working with a dolphin and his rider in Sanwight, trying to figure out if the telepathic communications between magical creatures and their riders could be *expanded* to be communication between all magical creatures. We haven't made any *significant* progress yet, but we are becoming good friends with Benjamin and his dolphin, Horace."

Joseph continued, "If we left now, we could meet with Benjamin and be back here within the forty-four hours. I *know* we can trust Benjamin and Horace. They wouldn't do anything to harm dragons. Maybe Benjamin knows something, and if not, maybe he can find out and then communicate with us. We haven't had any luck with telepathic communication between Horace and either Samantha or Spruce, but Samantha and Spruce have *both* been able to talk, at least briefly, with Benjamin. We'll see if we can strengthen that while we're there."

Clotilda said, "It's very clear that our youngest dragon riders are taking their research requirements very seriously. It's so helpful that you have all decided on researching telepathic communications. We certainly need that now. Nice work. You two head out, and whatever you do, *don't* put yourself anywhere that the Baron can find! Be sure you are back before the forty-four hours are over."

"We will," they chorused as they ran out of the arena.

"OK, that's it for now. Stay alert, and if anyone thinks of anything else we could try, please come see me *immediately.* Matilda and I will be trying to contact dragons and riders... although I must admit, we've developed them mainly between ourselves and not with other dragons and riders. That's something we will have to fix as soon as this is over. Leave it to the young to teach the old new tricks." She smiled and shook her head. "Oh, and Peter, as the senior non-dragon rider, you are in charge of our non-dragon-riding allies. See if you can find out anything from them. Also, get our signal fires lit. That should bring the closer dragons and riders home right away."

As the riders were filing out of the arena, Clotilda called to Emily, "Could you stay for a few minutes?"

Emily nodded. Gregory said he'd wait for her outside.

As soon as they were alone, Clotilda looked thoughtfully at Emily and then said, "As you know, dragons and their riders are always led, if possible, by a female purple and her rider. I hadn't meant to start your training quite so soon, but this crisis proves that we can't wait. From now on, I want you and Esmeralda to be our shadows—sitting next to us at all meetings, contributing your insights, and learning every detail of what it means to be a dragon leader.

Emily looked shocked, clasping her hands, looking at her feet, and finally looking back at Clotilda. Clotilda's eyes were so gentle that Emily calmed herself with a deep breath and answered, "I understand and I hope we prove worthy of this honor."

Clotilda smiled before saying, "Get out of here and plan your spying strategies with Gregory."

Emily left the arena thoughtfully, her mind awash with information. Gregory was waiting in the main courtyard and he and Emily made their arrangements for signals. Emily and Esmeralda would start their patrols tomorrow, giving Gregory time to get home. Plus, Emily and Esmeralda wanted time for some much-needed rest.

— 9 —

INTELLIGENCE GATHERING

Emily and Esmeralda slept well snuggled together under Esmeralda's purple quilt. The stone walls of the cave were getting colder as winter approached, but Esmeralda's nest was always warmed from the volcano below, so they were cozy. As the sun rose, they woke up eager to start their assigned task. Once the banishment went into effect and dragons could be shot on sight, they would have to limit their patrols to evening, but since that banishment hadn't yet started, Emily and Esmeralda figured they would spend today and part of tomorrow searching the Baron's lands as closely as possible, as long as Clotilda didn't need them for anything else. Emily had to admit that she was a little nervous about becoming a leader-in-training so soon after her graduation.

Emily headed into the dining hall for her breakfast. She already missed her friends, but she knew they were thrilled to have been given such important missions. Thanks to William and Thunder, dragons and their riders had already started returning to Havenshold. Emily was amazed at how smart and resourceful William was. To think that Anne and Joseph were already in Sanwight...they would have to be very careful indeed.

There were still thirty-six hours before the banishment went into effect, so everyone was doing all they could.

After conferring briefly with Clotilda and Matilda, Emily and Esmeralda packed up some provisions for the day and took to the skies. The Baron's land was just below Havenshold, but it was a vast holding. The Baron had managed to snatch up more land than anyone else and he had made himself very unpopular in the process. Emily thought to Esmeralda, *I wonder why all the other nobles are backing the Baron when they hate him so much?*

Esmeralda chuckled darkly. *Fear.*

Emily shuddered. *How horrible it must be to feel that you have to intimidate people to get them to support you. And how dreadful for those the Baron has holds over. Lives lived in fear really don't have much to recommend them.*

Esmeralda agreed. They flew in companionable silence until they were over the Baron's land.

Draconia was a very mountainous country. There was very little level ground and the altitude was such that not much grew, even on the level spots. But goats and sheep could always find grazing, and on the best, flattest spots—which mostly belonged to the Baron—it was possible to raise cattle.

Havenshold, nearly at the top of the mountain, was able to raise animals, but that was primarily because of all the work the dragon riders had done years ago when they first arrived to carve out spaces in the mountain. The dragon riders were given grain and other foods—from not only Draconia, but the neighboring lands as well—in trade for the energy the dragon riders were able to tap off the volcano and send where it was needed. *It was an equitable solution to the difficult problem of living near a volcano,* Emily thought. She had no idea why the Baron felt he needed to mess with it. How did he think the land would survive without the dragons? Did he think the riders would just keep on working for him? Didn't he realize how much the dragons meant to the riders?

Emily knew that talk had started about whether or not they should leave this world and once again seek out a new land. In fact, Clotilda had asked some of the more experienced riders to research that option. Emily sure hoped it didn't come to that. *People can be so stupid,* she thought, and she felt Esmeralda's affirmation.

It was a beautiful morning and Emily was enjoying the view. The Baron had put a lot into his land. Emily watched as people were out cleaning the fields now that winter was approaching, covering anything dormant with straw so it would not be damaged by the winter's snows and ice. Everything *looked* so peaceful. She saw small herds of sheep and cattle, but she had to agree there were nowhere near as many as before. *What could have happened to them?* Emily knew that no dragon rider would have taken them—that was simply a story dreamed up by the Baron—but would the Baron have killed off so many of his own livestock? Emily didn't think so. He was too greedy for that and cattle and sheep were a cash crop only if they were alive and healthy. So where could they have gone?

Esmeralda and Emily flew lower, just above ground level. All of a sudden they saw a tiny crack in the rocks. At least it looked tiny from the back of a dragon, but the ground around the crack had been trampled down. Only a *lot* of animals could have caused that. As they looked more closely, they noticed that the crack was the result of one rock having been pushed into a larger space.

Emily and Esmeralda flew around again, this time a bit higher, and were able to see behind the rock where there was a very narrow, but long, canyon. It was nearly invisible from the air unless you knew just where to look. The canyon was filled with sheep and cattle! *Here* was the answer to the mystery!

Emily and Esmeralda landed on a rock outcropping above the canyon and settled down to wait and watch. They couldn't be seen unless someone looked up from exactly the right spot.

After a few hours, Emily noticed a man on horseback approaching. It was Gregory's brother, Lance. He headed, without hesitation, into the canyon. The crack that had been left next to the rock was just large enough for a man and a horse to go through. Emily watched as Lance checked on the herd and made sure there was enough food and water. *What's that over in the corner?* thought Emily. Lance had picked up something strange. He held it up and Emily almost gasped. It was a pair of wings with a harness, wings that looked like dragon wings—at least from a distance.

Now Emily knew how the Baron had managed to hoodwink some of the other nobles into thinking that a dragon and rider were savaging the cattle. It had been Lance riding a horse with *wings* attached. She saw Lance trying to break the wings. He was going to destroy the evidence. Emily shouted and Esmeralda roared.

Lance looked up. For a brief moment Lance looked frightened, but then he saw who it was and laughed. "You' re no match for me!" Lance shouted at them. "Just wait until you see what my father has planned for *you.*" He took out his bow and nocked an arrow ready to loose it.

Emily shouted back, "Don't forget, the banishment hasn't begun yet! You can't shoot us or King Jacob will arrest you. And we've seen what you're doing."

Lance laughed again. "The King doesn't dare do anything against my father! He's terrified of what my father might do, so don't count on *that.* No one would believe *you* anyway. Now get out of here before I decide your ugly dragon has no business living!"

Emily was furious. Esmeralda was the most beautiful dragon in the world. Esmeralda sent calming thoughts to her. *Don't worry,* said Esmeralda. *He's just jealous because he was never picked be a candidate. He has to compensate for what he sees as a major failing.*

Emily was reassured by Esmeralda's thoughts and realized that Esmeralda was correct. *Let's get out of here and report back to Clotilda. We have a lot of new information.*

Emily and Esmeralda rose into the air and departed. Lance laughed, as if he'd scared them off. Emily told Esmeralda, *We'll be back tonight to move that rock. Then see how hard he's laughing when the cattle and sheep get out!* Esmeralda chuckled in response.

As soon as they were back at Havenshold, they went to Clotilda to report. "We found where the Baron's hiding the sheep and cattle he says he lost to dragons. We also know how he fooled some of his nobles—he had Lance riding a horse with wings attached to *look* like a dragon from a distance. Lance is cocky, *sure* that the Baron's hold is so strong over King Jacob that the King wouldn't dare to anything against the Baron."

Clotilda replied, "Excellent work, Emily. You and Esmeralda have managed to find *real* evidence of the Baron's subterfuge. Unfortunately, I suspect Lance has destroyed the evidence by now, but there's still the matter of all the sheep and cattle hidden in the canyon. It would be hard to refute that."

Emily smiled. "What if Esmeralda and I freed them tonight? The sheep and cattle would then be wandering all over in areas where they couldn't find food and water. That would mean that the Baron's men would have to spend a lot of time and energy rounding them up. Sheep are especially stubborn and would be *real* trouble to corral. If nothing else, it would distract the Baron for a while."

Clotilda thought for a minute, then nodded slowly. "Yes, that's a good idea, but remember, Lance was prepared to shoot you this morning. Be *very* careful. The banishment isn't in effect until tomorrow evening, so tonight *should* be safe, but I don't like the sound of Lance's boasting. They must have a serious hold over King Jacob even to *dare* threatening you. They'll be expecting something, now that Lance knows you found the missing animals. Wait until the moon has set and the night is at its darkest. And be *careful*."

Emily and Esmeralda spent the rest of the day training with Clotilda and Matilda. They had an early dinner and talked with other dragon riders who offered up their suggestions.

When they headed out, they flew very high so as not to be glimpsed from below. When they reached the canyon they could see a campfire. There were guards, just as she and the other riders had predicted. But they were *inside* the canyon? Was anyone on the outside?

Emily and Esmeralda looked around very carefully. There was one guard right outside the canyon entrance, but he appeared to have fallen asleep and his bow had slipped from his hands. *Sloppy work,* thought Emily. She and Esmeralda landed very quietly a few yards away and approached the rock. The plan was to have Esmeralda push the rock away with Emily still on her back, and then take off back into the sky, swoop over the canyon, and have Esmeralda send out a burst of flames—not enough to hurt anyone, just enough to spook the animals into running for the opening and scatter.

Emily and Esmeralda were nearly at the rock when the guard looked up. He hadn't been asleep after all. As he raised his bow, Esmeralda swung her tail around and knocked him sideways. They heard his arm snap as he hit a rock and he howled in pain.

Esmeralda and Emily worked quickly. They moved the rock and shoved it down the slope before anyone else could react.

They were back in the air and Esmeralda roared fire. True to form, the animals stampeded for the opening. Emily and Esmeralda looked down at the startled faces of the men at the campfire. Lance was among them.

Emily called down, "It isn't wise to mess with dragons!" She and Esmeralda headed back home.

— 10 —

RETALLIATION

The Baron was livid. Lance had just come into his father's office to report on Emily and Esmeralda's actions. The baron had been sitting behind his enormous marble desk, but he jumped up as he heard Lance's account and started pacing back and forth, holding his riding crop. The Baron cracked the whip within inches of Lance's face and yelled, "How could you let that little slip of a girl spot you? How could you let her get away? What were you thinking taking the *wings* out of hiding? Do you *have* a brain in your head?"

Lance stood still before his father. He knew this was the safest approach to take and that eventually his father would run out of steam.

The Baron continued. "And now our livestock is scattered all over the mountain where *wolves* will attack them! What were you thinking? Couldn't you even guard animals from *one woman?* How many of the livestock have you managed to round up? How many men is it taking? You are the *stupidest* man I know. If only you were *smart* like your brother."

Lance cringed. He hated the way his father always compared him to the *perfect* Gregory—only Gregory wasn't so perfect, but his father would never believe that. Gregory had tried to live up to his father's dreams for him, but the fact was, Lance knew Gregory was glad that the dragons hadn't picked him. Lance was sure that Gregory had some how communicated with the dragons and let them know that he didn't want to be a dragon rider. Lance never figured out how Gregory had done it, but because Gregory hadn't been chosen, their father had gone stark raving mad and was taking *everything* out on Lance.

Lance bowed his head before he finally replied. "I *know* I'm a disappointment to you, Father, but I *am* trying. I can see now that I should have waited to check on the livestock until the dragon banishment was in place. I never dreamed they would risk spying on us."

The Baron stopped pacing right in front of Lance and interrupted, "That's the whole problem, Lance! *You never think!* If only Gregory had been chosen, our lives would be so different. You're useless. Get out of my sight."

Lance quickly withdrew, glad to be out of the freezing cold dank office that his father seemed to love. At least he had been smart enough not to tell his father that his anger had gotten the better of him and caused him to let Emily know that his father had a hold over the King. If his father knew *that* secret was out, he would've been even more furious.

Lance thought his father was crazy, and this whole plan to get rid of dragons was never going to work—or so he secretly hoped.

As soon as Lance left, Henry—the gamekeeper—came in to report. Henry—a short, squat man with greying hair—swaggered when he walked, confident that the Baron couldn't run his holdings without him. "We've managed to round up most of the livestock. I think our losses are pretty small...that's the good part. The bad part is that we *can't* get them back into that canyon, because the blasted dragon knocked the boulder all the way down the mountain. I've had the men put them back into the regular herds and flocks, but that means if anyone comes snooping, they'll know that you haven't suffered the enormous losses you claimed."

"I know," replied the Baron. "That idiot son of mine just reported. Of course that *girl* will have reported everything at Havenshold. We have no choice now except to move ahead with our plans more quickly than we anticipated. I need to meet with the Sanwight nobles as soon as possible. I'll head out and cross the border secretly so that no one will know I'm gone. It will be up to you and the others to make it look as if I'm still here."

"Right you are, sir," said Henry. "My son, Sylvester, is working at Havenshold. If I could get word to him, maybe he would be willing to spy for us. He only works in the stables, but he hears a lot. There are others working for the dragon riders, but I don't know if we dare approach any of them. It is, after all, considered to be quite an *honor* to be a civilian employee of Havenshold."

"Well, try with Sylvester," said the Baron. "After all, we have someone watching every move King Jacob makes. It would be most helpful if we could also keep an eye on Clotilda."

"I'll do my best and get back with you. Don't you worry, sir, we'll stay true to you, get rid of the King, and make sure *you* are on the throne of Draconia before the New Year!" Henry said.

"Your loyalty will not go unrewarded, Henry," replied the Baron.

Henry bowed, a half smile, half scowl on his face, and left the room.

The Baron looked over his maps and reports, unaware that Gregory was watching him from the spy hole above.

Gregory had heard everything. He was so proud of Emily and Esmeralda and the havoc they had wreaked on his father's plans. Now Gregory needed to get out of here and up to Havenshold to report. *It shouldn't be too hard,* he thought. *All the men are still trying to cope with the livestock mess.*

Gregory hurried out of the castle, got on his horse—Lightning—and headed off in the direction of the Capitol. He wanted to be sure he wasn't being followed. After about an hour of what he hoped looked like aimless riding, Gregory was confident that he was alone. He made his way to Havenshold.

Once there, he was met in the main courtyard and immediately shown in to Clotilda's office. Gregory looked around in amazement. He was used to his father's office—built of stone and colder, more devoid of interest than Gregory could imagine. But here, Clotilda's office—also built of stone, carved out of the side of the volcano—had a light airy feeling. It was large enough to accommodate both Clotilda and Matilda, who at the moment was napping in a nest in the corner. All the walls were covered with paintings of dragon riders and their dragons. Some of these paintings were very old, and Gregory guessed that they showed the earliest dragon riders to come to this world, but some were very recent, including one of Emily and her classmates at the their graduation. He noticed Emily and Esmeralda were also there, off to the right side of Clotilda's desk. Gregory smiled at Emily who returned his smile, but Gregory's focus was brought back to the matter at hand as Clotilda motioned for him to be seated in the chair opposite her. As soon as he was seated he got right to the point.

"Emily and Esmeralda did a brilliant job! My father is absolutely furious. He yelled at Lance for the better part of the morning. The castle is upset and the men are having a hard time getting all the livestock back where they *ought* to be. Esmeralda fixed it so they can't be hidden away in that canyon again, so if anyone wants to make a check on the Baron's holdings, they'll discover he isn't missing all the livestock he said he was," Gregory said. He sat on the very edge of the chair, excited by this turn of events. Emily blushed as he reported.

"That is wonderful news," said Clotilda, taking a sip of hot coffee and pushing her glasses back up her nose. "Have you learned anything more?"

Gregory nodded. "I know for sure that my father is planning to depose King Jacob and get himself made king in his place. He wants to rule all of Draconia. It wouldn't surprise me if he's planning to rule the other nations as well...some kind of maniacal bid for an empire. He's gone absolutely crazy. I haven't yet found out what he and Henry hold they have over the King, but it must be powerful."

"I wish we knew what the hold was," said Clotilda, as she stood up and walked over to the map on the wall. "Then, we could neutralize it."

"I'll keep searching," replied Gregory. "Meanwhile, my father is forming some kind of alliance with the barons of Sanwight. Tonight, after dark, he's going to sneak across the border and meet with them."

"Excellent," answered Clotilda. "Emily, you and Esmeralda will follow him. Meanwhile, Anne and Joseph sent word that they were onto something. They won't be back before the banishment takes effect, but they'll return late tonight. I'm hoping they'll have information about whatever is going on in Sanwight."

"Well, if anyone can find out, those two can." Gregory said. He chuckled as he thought back to his childhood. "They loved to play detective when we were kids, and they were really good at it, remember Emily?" She smiled and nodded.

Clotilda smiled. "I can't believe the abilities of our newest group of dragon riders. But, talents arise when the situations demand. We certainly need *all* of them now. William, by the way, was able to make contact with all the riders within Draconia.

They're all safely back. He also spoke with our dragons in the other three nations. They agreed that they would stay where they were and gather information for us. That way, if we need to call on our allies, they'll be able to do that in a timely fashion."

Gregory stared up at Clotilda with wide eyes. He felt very much like a child as he realized the impact of what was happening around his world and that he was a part of it in a small way. He glanced at Emily and saw that she also was realizing the extent of all this.

Clotilda thought for a minute. "You're a volcanologist, right?" He nodded. "Do you think there's any way we can *divert* the power that's going to your father's lands to make his life a bit more...*uncomfortable?* Is there any way you could make that seem accidental?"

Gregory pondered for a few minutes. "I have a few ideas. Emily, you and Esmeralda have surveyed my father's lands the most recently, and you're the most devious pair I know...in a good way." He smiled at her. "What do you think?"

Emily took a moment and then said, "I'm sure that together we can come up with a plan.

Clotilda laughed. "If you want trickery and deviousness, go for a *purple* dragon every time. OK, you three are now working on a secret mission—*Depowering the Baron!*"

Gregory chortled. "Super." Then looking quickly at Emily and then back to Clotilda he continued, "I heard Emily was really angered by my brother's arrogance."

Clotida nodded. "It wasn't Esmeralda who was breathing fire when they returned! They would have gone back no matter what, so I figured it was wise to *authorize* it. I'm so glad it worked out. Their planning was brilliant and wonderfully executed. Best of all, no one got seriously hurt."

Emily blushed at the comment and looked down at her lap.

Gregory said, "I'm just not sure what to make of Lance. One minute I think he's working hand-and-glove with my father, and the next he's just being dragged along. Only time will tell what his true character is, but he has a wicked temper when he's being teased." Gregory shook his head, then straightened. He'd forgotten a vital part of information. "I have one more important piece of information for you."

"Goodness," said Clotilda. "You've already told us so much."

"Remember I said that my father had a spy close to the King?" said Gregory. "Well, I *don't* know who that is, but I *do* know that they're going to try to get Sylvester to spy on us. They think that because Sylvester is Henry's son that he'll do whatever his father wants, but I know that isn't true. Sylvester and I spent many hours together as children, complaining about how our fathers wanted us to be something other than who we were in order to fulfill *their* dreams. Henry wanted Sylvester to take over as gamekeeper of my father's lands, just as my father wanted me to become a dragon rider. Sylvester wanted no part of that. All he ever wanted was to care for dragons and other magical creatures. That's why he applied to work here. He loves his work and he *loves dragons.* He even told me that some of the dragons talk to him telepathically. I don't think Sylvester has ever told anyone here that, but he and I still meet to chat and support each other. I think if you talk with him *before* his father does that you'll have a double-agent."

"Excellent!" said Clotilda. "I'll meet with him immediately. Now you, Emily, and Esmeralda start figuring out how to shift the Baron's power supply. And Emily, stop back here when you're done so we can compare notes. We are deeply indebted to you, Gregory."

"My pleasure," he answered. Emily nodded as they left.

— 11 —

SPIES AND DOUBLE AGENTS

While Emily and Esmeralda had been hunting for the Baron's missing livestock, Anne and Joseph rode their dragons to just inside the Sanwight border. Joseph leaped off Spruce as Anne gracefully dismounted from Samantha. Spruce and Samantha enjoyed rolling in the grass as Joseph reached out telepathically to Benjamin, their dolphin rider contact.

As soon as he'd connected with Benjamin, he told Anne, "Benjamin says he can be here in a half hour and he will have horses for us. That way we can ride to the dolphin rider's home without attracting undo attention."

"Sounds great," replied Anne. She liked being out on a mission, especially one of this importance.

Joseph sat down on the grass next to Spruce and began idly scratching Spruce in his hard-to-reach spots, but Joseph was soon restless. He stoodm trying to see further, wondering how long it would be before Benjamin arrived.

Anne, sitting on the grass by Samantha, laughed as she watched him. "You never sit still for a minute, do you?" she said.

"Well," proclaimed Joseph, "this is important and we don't have much time before we have to be back at Havenshold."

"I know," said Anne, as she ran her fingers through her short blond hair. "But Benjamin said it would take a half hour and your pacing around won't make the clock go any faster."

Joseph laughed at himself. "I guess I am a bit anxious and you know I never did like sitting still. Oh, look, I see a cloud of dust ahead."

Anne looked where Joseph was pointing and soon they could make out Benjamin riding toward them with two horses in tow.

Benjamin stopped well away from the two dragons and Anne and Joseph went over to him. Benjamin was nearly six feet tall with a very slender build. He had jet black hair and sported a beard and mustache. Like Anne and Joseph, he was in his early twenties. He raised an arm in greeting. "Hi," he called out. "I was surprised to get your message. Has something happened?"

Anne and Joseph quickly brought Benjamin up to speed about the Baron's ultimatum.

"Gads," said Benjamin. "I was just hoping to show you around a bit and see if you could communicate with either Horace or any of the other dolphins or riders, but this is really serious. Let's get to The Corral—our home—and we can talk this out."

The three of them mounted up after telling Spruce and Samantha to be careful and to follow them telepathically. Soon they rode into the capitol of Sanwight and reached the bay where the dolphin riders and their dolphins lived.

"Wow!" exclaimed Joseph and Anne together. Joseph continued, "This is really cool! You practically live in the water with your dolphins just as we live in volcanic caves with our dragons."

Benjamin laughed. "Well, you may have it a bit easier, since both you and your dragons can live in the air. Our dolphins need to stay wet, so we end up spending a lot of time in the water, but obviously we all still need to breathe air. Nevertheless we like our spot here and it works well for us. You can see the sloped surfaces here which allow our dolphins to get really close. We also have floating hammocks so we can sleep with them as well.

"But let's find out what we need to do, as your time is limited," continued Benjamin. "Why are you here and how can we help?"

Joseph asked, "How are things here in Sanwight? Do you hear anything which might relate to what the Baron is doing in Draconia?"

"Funny you should ask," answered Benjamin, as they all sat around the edge of a large pool. Horace hovered near enough for Benjamin to rub him. "There is a large group of nobles who have become dissatisfied with the status quo. They're putting pressure on King Stefan to *insist* on more energy from Draconia, as well as higher prices for their fish. They've also pointed out that dolphins are not in the same category as dragons, gryphons, or unicorns. Dolphins aren't magical, nor as supposedly vicious as dragons and gryphons."

At this comment both Spruce and Samantha spoke telepathically to their riders with loud snorts of disbelief. Joseph passed their comments onto Benjamin. "That's total hogwash. Neither dragons nor gryphons are vicious."

"I agreed," answered Benjamin, "and neither are unicorns. I think, personally, that they want more land. The nobles aren't fishermen. They've risen to power because of their mercantile abilities, but I think they see nobles in other lands—such as Draconia—who are large land owners and think that somehow those nobles are superior to them.

"And it gets worse," continued Benjamin. "While it's *only* the nobles who are sewing seeds of discontent, they've managed to get King Stefan stirred up. Apparently, they're talking about some kind of *merging* of the nations, or at least a very close alliance. If they get King Stefan's support, then they also will get the use of Sanwight's army—an army, I might add, that's much larger than what a seafaring nation would seem to need. They could be a real threat."

Anne asked, "Why does Sanwight have such a large army?"

"Funny you should ask," said Benjamin as he reached for a cool drink and offered some to Anne and Joseph as well. "Our population is really stratified. We have the fishermen of course, and those families train up their children to follow in their footsteps—which they usually do—but with the mercantile nobles, there are a lot of younger siblings with nothing to do as the businesses pass from father to eldest child. So someone got the bright idea of sending all these young nobles into the military. Now we have an oversized army just looking for trouble. They want a war so they can get war spoils."

Joseph, who'd been bouncing lightly from foot to foot in agitation, said, "I heard that Baron Geldsmith has been spending a *lot* of time in Sanwight. Do you know anything about that?"

Benjamin answered quickly, "Yes, we've been wondering about that also. He's even bought a house here and attends royal functions as one of King Stefan's *friends.* I don't know what he's been saying to King Stefan—as I am not invited to such functions—but you better believe it isn't favorable to dragons or King Jacob."

Benjamin continued, "We've noticed that something funny is going on at the Baron's Sanwight house. There now are Sanwight guards stationed *around* the house, and no one is allowed to go in without some kind of pass. I haven't been able to find out anything more. We've tried to snoop a bit when we were there, but we were unsuccessful at discovering anything. I've had my dolphin riders spying on the place, because I am not happy about it at all. What right does the Baron have to use

Sanwight guards? After what you have told me, we are going to work even harder to find out what's going on.

"And if that weren't enough," added Benjamin, "someone is stirring up discontent among the fishermen, planting the idea in the fishermen's heads that they could get *more* fish and hence more *money* if they used nets—but of course those nets are *highly* dangerous for dolphins. The fisherman are starting to think they don't need us."

Benjamin, Anne, and Joseph each pondered the situation for a bit before Anne said, "You've given us a lot to think about. I think we'd better get back to Spruce and Samantha so we can report all this to Clotilda."

"Sounds as if you have as many problems as we do," remarked Joseph. "Sure am glad that we can communicate telepathically. Please keep us informed and we'll do the same."

"For sure," said Benjamin.

With that the three of them rode back to the dragons. It was nightfall, and thankfully a moonless night, but even so the flight back to Havenshold would be risky. The clock had run out on the temporary truce and the Baron could now shoot to kill.

"Be careful, you four," said Benjamin.

With that. Anne, Joseph, Samantha, and Spruce took off into the night.

The next morning, Clotilda woke up, eager for a new day to discover how to handle the Baron's treason. Joseph and Anne had returned from Sanwight in the middle of the night, so she let them sleep for a bit, but called a meeting with them for 9:00 a.m. in the large hall so that Spruce and Samantha could be there also.

"Let's hear your report," said Clotilda. Emily was at her side, eager for her friends' report.

Anne said, "We met with Benjamin and Horace. What they had to tell us was very disquieting." The two of them then related everything they had learned while in Sanwight.

Joseph concluded the report by saying, "Benjamin realizes—as apparently their King doesn't—that the balance in our world is delicate, and without that balance we would end up in a world wide conflict. If Sanwight and Draconia become closer allies or a single nation, then Forbury and Granvale will be angered. It isn't in *anyone's* best interest for this plot to continue. Benjamin and his fellow dolphin riders are doing their best to stem the tide of dissent."

Clotilda started pacing the hall to give herself time to think. Finally she said, "It seems ours is not the only country where the value of the animal rider bond is being questioned. We haven't heard any rumors out of Forbury or Granvale, so I certainly hope this attitude hasn't spread to either of them. As far as our ambassadors can gather, everything is going along as usual in both countries. But then, they don't have Baron Geldsmith visiting them."

Emily said, "I've looked over the latest reports from both Forbury and Granvale and everything seems to be calm and normal in both countries.

Anne said, "There's absolutely *no* doubt that all this trouble began when the Baron bought a house and started spending time there. His drive for power is poisoning more than just *our* land. Sanwight is the smallest of the four nations. In the Baron's eyes, I'll bet it's the easiest to manipulate."

"Thank you, both," said Clotilda with gracious nods. "And thank you for staying longer, even though that put both of you at greater risk. Did you notice anything last night when you flew back, now that the banishment is in effect?"

Joseph answered, "The Baron has men stationed on the highest parts of his land with lookouts, watch fires, and plenty of soldiers. They spotted us briefly as we flew over, but their arrows were ineffectual as we were too high to be reached."

Spruce commented telepathically to them all, *As if those puny soldiers could do anything against us!* Samanatha concurred with a snort and Esmeralda chuckled.

"But if they got anywhere near our landing field, it could be trickier, especially for the rider," Emily said. "Even with our riding habits, we're vulnerable. Our dragons are more than equal to the task of protecting us, but I think it would be wise to have some drills to remind dragons and riders how to fly defensively, and how to protect each other. Heaven forbid if the soldiers shot flaming arrows and one pierced a wing."

Clotilda said, after a thought, "Let's set up a schedule for dragon drills, including fast takeoffs and landings, and higher flying, which means that riders need to learn to acclimatize themselves to higher altitudes and less oxygen. The infirmary has some herbs that can help with that." She turned to Emily and said, "Will you see to that?" Emily nodded and Clotilda turned back to Anne and Joseph saying, "Thank you both again. You may resume your normal duties. I'll call you if I have any further questions."

As Anne, Joseph, Spruce, and Samantha left, Clotilda was deep in thought. She asked Emily to summon both Sylvester and Gregory. She wanted to see how Sylvester felt about being made a double agent. It would be worthwhile to talk with Gregory as well to see how he felt about returning to his father's castle as a spy.

"Good morning, gentlemen," Clotilda said. "I'm so glad you could come to confer with us. Gregory, the information you brought us yesterday was absolutely invaluable."

Gregory said, "I'm glad. Someone has to stop my crazy power-hungry—dare I say—*deranged* father."

"And mine," said Sylvester. "I got a message from him last night by a raven. He hinted that he needed me at home for something really urgent, but Gregory had already told me what he heard from my father. I will never be a party to anything that would hurt dragons *or* riders!"

Clotilda and Emily both smiled as Clotilda said, "I understand that you have a special relationship with some of the dragons, Sylvester. Can you tell me about that?"

Sylvester looked around. He twisted his hands together, as if he might be in trouble. When he spoke, his voice was quiet. "Well, I haven't done anything outside of my job, but *part* of my job is helping to nurse injured dragons, and when a rider is working on his or her dragon to mend an injury, I help by just holding the injured part or stroking the dragon to keep them calm. I was doing this one time, oh, a couple years back, just thinking soothing thoughts, and I was surprised to hear the dragon *in my head!* It was Hans's Fire Dancer. She spoke back to me, thanking me for distracting her from what Hans was doing to her tail. She asked my name and how I came to be there, and we chatted away."

Clotilda looked at him with wide eyes. "You've spoken tele-pathically to a dragon. You do know that that rarely happens, don't you?"

"Yes, Ma'am," replied Sylvester, twisting his hands even harder and staring at the floor. "I didn't mean any disrespect."

Clotilda laughed. "Quite the contrary. You were showing the dragon the *greatest* respect, and for that you were honored by having the dragon speak to you. That is amazing. Dragons and their own riders communicate that way, and sometimes drag-ons will communicate with riders other than their own, or other non-dragon riders whom their rider is very close to. It seems this dragon-person connection can be a lot stronger than any of us had any reason to suspect. Both of you have now been touched by dragons. That's not only a rare, but an incredible experience."

Sylvester gained confidence now that he understood Clotilda was pleased with this information. He spoke louder with a smile. "Yes, Ma'am. The first time it happened, it nearly knocked me over. I looked up at Hans as he worked on Fire Dancer's tail and he just smiled. Since then, it's happened several more times—always when I was helping to ease a dragon's pain—and each time I've been totally awed." His face hardened and he slammed a fist into his open palm. "There's no way I could *ever* hurt a dragon! Most of the riders have been really great to me as well, even letting me go for rides with them occasionally. I don't think most of Draconia has any idea how *important* you all are to the nation."

"Thank you, Sylvester," replied Clotilda. "What we wanted to know is if you are willing to do something much riskier to help *us*."

"I am," replied Sylvester without a moment's hesitation. "But what can I do? I'm no soldier."

"We'd like you to accept your father's offer, but not in the way he thinks. We'd like you to become a double agent for us. However, if you agree, I must warn you that it could be very dangerous if your father or the Baron finds out," said Clotilda.

"I can do it." He turned to Gregory. "Remember how we used to play spies? We had lots of practice and never got caught. I know this is no game, though. This is important," replied Sylvester.

Clotilda said, "And what about you, Gregory? Are you going to return to your home and spy for us?"

"Yes," said Gregory. "Definitely. I can give Sylvester a ride home if he wants, so he can visit his father this afternoon, and we can set this all in motion."

"I'll be sure you have the afternoon off, Sylvester. Please report to me when you return. Meanwhile, you might let your father know that this banishment has us all very worried. Don't make us sound too weak or stupid, but make him think that we're trying to figure out how to do our duty *and* carry out our obligations to Draconia without having the dragons leave Havenshold. Let him know that we're still trying to recall all the dragons. That way, if he gets wind of dragons flying at night, he'll think they're coming here, rather than patrolling. Can you do this?"

"Yes," said Sylvester. "Neither of our fathers have ever seen us as men in our own right, so we've gotten very good at deceiving them."

Clotilda continued. "I would also like to have you work on your telepathic communications with Emily and Esmeralda. I know, Gregory, that you have spoken briefly with Esmeralda. Let's see if we can strengthen that so that Esmeralda can monitor you both in case you need assistance."

Emily, Gregory, and Sylvester all nodded.

"OK then," replied Clotilda. "You have your orders. Keep me informed and good luck to you all."

— 12 —

BARRÍCADE

It was early afternoon when Gregory and Sylvester headed out together after working with Emily and Esmeralda on telepathic skills. Esmeralda could speak with both Gregory and Sylvester at short distances, which was excellent progress. Sylvester rode one of the few Havenshold horses and Gregory rode Lightning. Not many horses were kept at Havenshold, since they tended to be afraid of dragons, but Sylvester had trained a few so that they tolerated dragons. Gregory was a bit distracted by his telepathic lessons and he could still feel Esmeralda encouraging him to maintain contact.

Gregory and Sylvester had decided to split up when they got closer to the Baron's castle, because Gregory didn't want it known that he had been to Havenshold.

The two rode in companionable silence for awhile until Gregory started. "What's that up ahead?"

Sylvester looked and said, "It looks like some kind of blockade. Those are your father's men."

"Quick," said Gregory. "You get down and head over to see what's going on. Lightning and I are going to have to try to go around. See you at the castle."

"Good luck," replied Sylvester as he got down. He watched as Gregory headed off into the woods and then he walked forward to the blockade. "Hello. What's going on?" he called as he approached.

"Baron's orders," said the assistant gamekeeper, George, as he nodded at Sylvester. "No one goes into Havenshold anymore without *written* authorization from the Baron. Of course, anyone can come out, but they won't be able to go back."

"But, I *live* and *work* there," said Sylvester. "Surely I can return. My father just asked to see me."

"Maybe yes, maybe no," said George. "Our orders are pretty clear. You may certainly come out, and maybe that's why your father sent for you. He didn't want you *trapped* in there. Things could get nasty with no supplies being delivered, and we have orders to shoot *any* dragon who tries to run the blockade."

"I can't believe this. Did the King order this?" asked Sylvester.

George grinned. "I don't think the King rightly knows what's going on. He pretty much does what the Baron says these days."

"Well, I don't want to lose my job. Do you know where my father is?" asked Sylvester.

"He's supposed to relieve me in an hour or so," said George.

"Fine then," said Sylvester. "I'll just wait right here on *this* side of the blockade."

"Suit yourself," said George, "but you better think about which side you want to be on when the Baron takes over."

Sylvester thought to himself, *What an idiot, saying things like that aloud*. He found himself a rock and made himself as comfortable as he could while his horse grazed on scrub grass. He'd let his father come to him.

Meanwhile, Gregory was circling through the woods, hoping to find a way to break through the blockade. He was dismayed to see that his father had blocked all the roads up the mountain, even the small trails that were rarely used.

Esmeralda, can you hear me?

Loud and clear, she thought back to him. *And Emily can hear you through me. What's up?*

I'm not sure, but there are blockades everywhere. I'll keep you posted.

Gregory decided to take one of the least known trails and then say that he'd been hunting in the woods beyond, as this trail also branched off to the Capitol. Being found here shouldn't make it conclusive that he'd been at Havenshold.

There was just one guard on this small trail and he nodded as soon as he saw that it was Gregory. "Afternoon, sir."

Gregory was saddened to see that it was Thomas, one of the guards who had been nicest to Gregory when he was a boy and always had taken time to play with him. Thomas was a kind and gentle man, with kids and grandkids of his own. There was no one to blame except his father.

"Hi, Thomas," answered Gregory. "What are you doing out here?"

"Baron's orders," replied Thomas. "No one's being allowed to go up to Havenshold. The Baron doesn't want them to get any supplies. I don't understand, but I'm just following orders, as always, sir."

"Right," said Gregory. "You won't have any trouble with me. I was just out checking on game and ended up following a stag that I then lost in the woods. Won't the people in Havenshold be hurting if they don't get fresh food? There are more than just dragons up there."

"I don't know, sir. truly I don't," answered Thomas. "My oldest granddaughter just got hired up there to work in the kitchens. She was so proud, since as you know, those jobs are good and very hard to come by. We're really worried about her."

"Well, don't worry, Thomas," said Gregory. "My father may be strict, but he'd allow people to leave so they won't starve. It's the dragons he wants."

Thomas nodded. "We have orders to shoot any dragon trying to break the blockade, but...I don't know if I could do that. They're such beautiful creatures, and your father's livestock has all returned now anyway, so what's the point?"

"What's the point, indeed," said Gregory. "I guess I'd better get home and try to find that out. Take care, Thomas. I'm sure your granddaughter will be just fine. After all, the riders have always taken very good care of everyone at Havenshold."

"You're right there, sir," said Thomas. "Have a good day!"

Gregory thought, *Esmeralda and Emily. Did you get that? We did. What a mess!*

Gregory continued home, where he found his father pacing in his office. "What's going on, Father?" asked Gregory. "I came across a blockade on my way back from hunting."

"I'm going to take care of those dragons." The Baron snarled as he spoke. "I know they're up there laughing at me! We caught sight of a couple dragons flying back late last night, out of range of our arrows. They're taunting me and *not* obeying the banishment."

"Well, I hear all your livestock is back, so maybe the dragons are not at fault," said Gregory, maintaining an innocent expression.

"That's beside the point!" snapped his father. "These dragons think they *rule* the land and they *have to be stopped.* I'm going to make sure they have no supplies and that they can't leave."

"So, *you* ordered the barricade? Does King Jacob know?" asked Gregory, the innocent tone to his voice giving way the slightest bit to his anger. His father didn't seem to notice.

"The King left *me* to take care of this situation. He gave me total control and I'm just exercising my rights as the commander of this operation. I'm sure the King has the utmost confidence in my ability to handle this," answered the Baron. His eyes were slits as he looked at his eldest son, but he didn't say anything else.

"I'm sure he does," said Gregory. Inside, Gregory was smoldering. His father was beyond hope.

"Just remember," his father continued, pacing back and forth across his office. "I'm doing this all for you. You're my heir and I want you to inherit a strong holding—one that's ruled properly and isn't being overrun by *dragons.* I'm sure the dragons are hunting in our forests, and I know that if left unchecked, they'll start ravaging the countryside. King Jacob has always been too weak. Just because he was once a rider doesn't give him the right to excuse their arrogant ways. They must be banished from our world and I'm going to see that that happens."

"What about the innocent people up in Havenshold, people who work there? Won't they suffer from the blockade as well?" asked Gregory.

"That's their worry." The Baron had white spit gathered at the corners of his mouth. "They never should have taken jobs there in the first place. I know that Havenshold has a good reputation as an employer, but it's unnatural to work for such *creatures.* No self-respecting person would do so. It is high time they decided where their loyalties lie. They can always just walk away. We aren't stopping anyone who wants to leave."

Oh, so that's your answer, thought Gregory, but he didn't want to anger his father further. "It seems you have it all figured out then."

"Yes, I do. Remember, I'm doing this *all for you.* You need to start taking more responsibilities here. You should be leading the men in this blockade—stepping up, taking command. Lance is doing much more than you. He really loves this land."

Gregory simmered. He said, "I'm glad that he does and that he's such a help to you. I told you, I have my studies. I really think

I can make a difference—not only to our nation but our entire world—if I learn more about how our volcano works. There are lots of people who can raise cattle and sheep, but not everyone can become a volcanologist. Why can't you see that?"

"We don't need that volcano! We can make our own energy. I don't know what you're making such a fuss over." His father waved his hand, his face turning red.

"If the dragon riders decide to change the power they're providing, you might just see how much you owe to them," snapped Gregory. He quickly regretted his words. "*Truly* Father, I think we *do* need to understand the volcano. Right now, only the dragon riders know anything about the workings of it. Do you want them to have that kind of power? If there were an eruption, your lands would be in the *most* jeopardy. I'm only trying to be sure that *our* holdings stay safe."

The Baron thought for a minute. "Well, I'm not happy about the riders' control of the volcano, that's for sure. That's way too much power for them to hold, so maybe you do have a point. But remember, no matter *how* much you study, in the end you must become the next baron."

"Yes, Father," said Gregory. "I'm your heir."

"Now, go read your books, or whatever it is you do all day. I have a kingdom to run," said the Baron, stomping back to his desk.

Gregory gratefully and hastily left. He tried to communicate with Emily, but he received no response. *Damn, I must be too far away. We need more practice, or at least I do.*

— 13 —

CONNIVING BARON

As soon as Gregory left, Baron Geldsmith called for Henry. The Baron had to get to Sanwight tonight. He would leave the castle secretly as soon as it was dark, but first he needed to talk things over with Henry. "Henry," said the Baron. "As we discussed this morning, we need to move the timing of our take-over up. By now the King has surely gotten word that my livestock was not *really* devoured by dragons. He could rebel, and so could the other nobles who weren't very happy with my move. I know too many secrets for *open* rebellion, but I don't think we can delay our plans any longer."

Henry nodded. "I think you're right. I've noticed some of our men getting restless, especially with the enforcement of the blockade. Some of them have family members working at Havenshold and they're worried about their safety. The sooner the dragons are gone,and you're on the throne, the better."

"I'm going to head to Sanwight tonight," replied the Baron, "and arrange for the next step in our plans. I want you to be in charge in my absence. Maintain the blockade, watch out for any weaknesses among our own people, and...I'd like you to keep an eye on Gregory. Unobtrusively, of course, but I'm not happy with the way he is reacting to all this."

Henry nodded. "I'm heading up to the main barricade now to relieve George for a few hours, but I'll be back before you leave. George sent word that Sylvester is waiting there for me there."

"Excellent," said the Baron. "I'll check in with you before I leave. Hope you have better luck with Sylvester than I did with Gregory."

Henry departed and headed out to the barricade so that George could have a break. When he reached the barricade, Henry saw that Sylvester was sitting on a rock on the Havenshold side of the barricade. Henry checked in with George. "Is everything going according to plan," he asked.

"So far," replied George. "We've turned back three supply wagons. The drivers weren't happy. They wanted to know what they were supposed to do with all that fresh produce, as no one eats as much as dragons and their riders. I told them I didn't care what they did with it, but they weren't going up the road."

"Nice work," answered Henry. "Anything else?"

George said, "There've been a few folks coming down, thinking they would have a day off in the city, but when they found out that they wouldn't be allowed to go back once they crossed the barricade, they just turned around and returned to Havenshold. Even Sylvester wouldn't cross the line. Said he didn't want to lose such a great job, but he knew you wanted to see him. He's just been sitting there for the last hour."

"OK," said Henry. "You take a break and I'll keep an eye on things, but I promised the Baron I would be back to the castle by nightfall, so be sure you're back at dusk."

"Will do." George rode back to the castle while Henry went over to talk to Sylvester.

"So, you didn't want to leave Havenshold?" asked Henry.

Sylvester answered, "It is a great job with good pay. I sure don't want to lose that. You sent a message that you wanted to see me, so I waited."

"The Baron and I need your help. I know it's a good job you have, but I know you also know where your *true* loyalties lie." As he said this, Henry watched Sylvester, who just nodded amiably. Henry realized he had never been able to read his son. He didn't know what Sylvester was really thinking. He continued nonetheless. "The Baron and I want to know what's going on up at Havenshold. We need to know how the dragons and riders are reacting and what their plans are. Are you willing to help keep us informed?" asked Henry.

Sylvester looked deep in thought, his brows knitted together. He looked up at his father. "I wouldn't want to get into trouble."

Henry ground his teeth. Was this really *his* son? So worried about getting into trouble? Sylvester had always been an amiable boy, eager to please, but he also had a stubborn streak—as Henry had found out to his great surprise when Sylvester refused to train in his footsteps. Sylvester was a peace lover and would not even stand up for himself in a fight. Henry—whose fists were always swinging at the slightest insult—never understood this. He proceeded cautiously.

"Oh, I wouldn't ask you to sneak around or eavesdrop," he said quickly. "I wouldn't want you to do anything like that. Just let me know what you find out in the course of your duties. For instance, what was their initial reaction to the banishment?"

Sylvester thought for a minute. "Oh, well, the dragon riders are all nervous and trying to figure out how to care for their dragons as well as the people who work at Havenshold. They're nice guys, father, just trying to work out how to look after themselves. They're hoping the King will come to his senses soon, but until then, they're just hunkering down and working on rationing, figuring out what supplies they have, that kind of thing."

"Very good," said Henry. *This is going to be easier than we thought. They are all a bunch of milksops, like my son.* "That's all we needed to know. Just send me a message by raven if anything changes, or to update me on how they're reacting to the barricade, will you?"

"I guess that couldn't hurt," said Sylvester. "You know, we *need* the dragons and their riders. They'd never harm anyone."

"Well, maybe," said his father, "but this is the *King's* wish, and we have to serve our King," said Henry, his voice laden with sarcasm.

"Is that all you wanted, Father? I'm supposed to be back at Havenshold by dinnertime."

"Yes, just send me a message by raven *each evening,*" answered Henry.

"OK, Father." Sylvester turned and rode back to Havenshold.

Henry watched at the barricade until George returned. Then he headed back to the castle to report to the Baron. "Sylvester doesn't want any trouble. He'll send us a raven every evening to let us know how the dragon riders are reacting to our embargo and what they're doing. He just doesn't have it *in* him to be a spy, but he'll report honestly to me. He's a good boy."

"Thanks, Henry," said the Baron. "I appreciate that. Good to know that they're all more worried about their survival than anything else. That way they won't try anything stupid, like trying to get to the King." He chuckled. "I'm off now. I'll be back tomorrow evening once I've set everything in motion in Sanwight."

Henry said, "And I'll keep everything moving smoothly here. Good luck."

The Baron departed for Sanwight. He went alone and rode swiftly. He was at his home in Sanwight before light. He immediately requested an appointment with King Stefan, and was told that the King could see him at noon. Meanwhile, he arranged a meeting with the Sanwight rebel nobles.

As soon as they were all gathered, the Baron addressed them. "We need to move up our timetable. The King is getting suspicious. Unfortunately, my livestock—which was supposed to have been dragon fodder—was found, so now the excuse to banish the dragons is null and void. That'll just make our job harder. But, if we strike quickly, we can take Draconia by surprise."

Terence, the leader of the noble rebels, said, "That *sounds* good, but what assurances do we have that after we help you gain Draconia's throne that you're actually going to *keep* your promises of alliances and greater energy allotments from the volcano?"

"I'm meeting with King Stefan at noon," replied the Baron, "and I'm going to propose that the alliance be ratified by the announcement of the engagement of his daughter, Priscilla, to my son, Gregory. That way, she'll become Draconia's queen once my son inherits the kingship."

"Will your son agree?" asked Terence.

The Baron said, "My son will do what he's told. All you need to do is gather your forces so that when I send word, the invasion can begin. Now, I'm off to meet with the King."

Terence nodded. "We'll be ready."

The Baron headed off to Sanwight Palace.

Once he was ushered in to see King Stefan, Baron Geldsmith began his plan to turn the King to his way of thinking, and to get him to agree to the banishment and slaughter of not only the dragons, but also the dolphins. The Baron secretly hoped, eventually, the gryphons and unicorns would go as well.

"Good afternoon," said the Baron. "It's a *pleasure* to see you again."

"Likewise," replied King Stefan. "How can I help you?"

"We're getting very close to the time for the invasion of Draconia. I have just met with your *sympathetic* nobles and they're getting preparations well in hand. I thought *now* might be a good time for us to announce the engagement of Priscilla to Gregory."

"Priscilla is very young—only twelve-years-old—but she thinks your Gregory is most handsome. So yes, I agree," said King Stefan. "We can have a lavish party once you are on Draconia's throne, but the announcement can be made public now."

"Thank you, your majesty," answered the Baron. "I know that you, like me, want to *rid* this world of these *evil* creatures who have such holds over us. First the dragons, then the dolphins, and hopefully, *eventually,* we'll get rid of gryphons and unicorns as well."

"Yes, those bonds are *unnatural,*" said King Stefan, shuddering. "The special privileges they get are harmful. They don't have to pay taxes, and the fishermen hate not being able to fish with nets. And what services do they provide? Nothing we couldn't do for *ourselves.*"

"I couldn't agree with you more," answered the Baron. "You've stated the case succinctly and accurately. It's a real pleasure to work with such a *right* thinker. I look forward to the time when we can join our kingdoms *against* Forbury and Granvale. Our world *will* be pure again!"

King Stefan nodded. "Is there anything else you need?"

"Not at this time," replied the Baron. "I need to return to my castle before I'm missed. I'll send word as soon as we're ready for the invasion. Again, thank you. I look forward to our alliance."

The Baron left the Palace and rode swiftly toward home as night approached.

— 14 —

DÍSCOVERÍES

As soon as he finished his breakfast, Baron Geldsmith summoned Gregory to his office. "Son, I have wonderful news," he began with a smile. "I've found you a bride."

Gregory looked startled. "I didn't know I needed one."

"Don't be absurd," said the Baron. "Of course you do. It's your duty as heir to marry well. I've just returned from Sanwight. King Stefan has agreed that his eldest daughter, Priscilla, will wed you. You're fortunate to have such a lovely and well-placed bride."

"But, Father," Gregory said. "She's only twelve-years-old! Nowhere near old enough to marry."

"Well, of course, the marriage will be in *name only* for a few years, but I'm sure you can respect that. It will *align* us with Sanwight."

"Shouldn't it be King Jacob's son, Rupert, who marries her? They're the same age, and normally kings marry their daughters off to princes, not baron's sons. Is there something I should know?" asked Gregory, standing rigidly and frowning.

"Nothing you need to worry about," answered his father. "Let's just say that King Jacob may not *always* be on Draconia's throne. There are no promises that Rupert would succeed him, anyway. That isn't how Draconia's kings are selected."

"What?" asked Gregory. "The son of the reigning King has *always* been given first priority to succeed—whether or not he's a dragon rider—and I would have thought you of all people would prefer a *non*-dragon rider. If Rupert choses not to succeed, then the next King will be chosen from among the *strongest* dragon riders."

"Not necessarily," answered his father with a smirk. "But let's not worry about those details now. Suffice it to say, King Stefan was very happy when I proposed you as his future son-in-law, so it's all set. It's a great honor for you. I knew you would be pleased."

Gregory said nothing for a few minutes, shifting his weight from one leg to the other as he thought. He knew how important it was to appear to agree. Finally, Gregory said, "I'm just *overwhelmed* by this news, Father. I had no idea you were seeking such an alliance, or such a marriage, for me. Thank you for always doing your very best for me."

"I'm so glad that you see that. I haven't always been sure that you were in agreement with my plans for you, but I've tried to be understanding about your desire to study volcanology, at least until it was time for you to start taking over some of the heavy responsibilities. Soon though, you'll have to settle down to some really hard work. I need to train you properly."

"Yes, Father," replied Gregory. "I understand. And I'm always ready to do what's *best* for our lands and our nation." Gregory thought, *But what is best is not you, nor your visions of power and destruction.*

"That's wonderful," said his father. "Well, I just wanted to give you the good news. I have a lot to do and I'm sure you do also."

"For certain," answered Gregory.

As soon as Gregory was out of the room he headed quickly to his own chambers, gathered up everything he cared about, stuffed it all in a couple large saddle bags, and headed to the stables. He was glad that everyone was out working. He was able to saddle Lightning and leave without having to answer any questions. *Everyone must be manning those stupid barricades,* he thought as he rode out.

He headed up the road toward Havenshold. Since no one was being allowed in, Gregory had to think fast. Obviously he couldn't get a note from his father allowing him past the barricade, because his father would lock him up in his room if he knew that Gregory was leaving. Too many of his father's plans depended on having a dutiful son ready to jump as high as he said. This marriage proposal was the last straw. Gregory really didn't think he would gain much more useful information staying at the castle. He needed to get out where he could really *help* the dragons and their riders.

But, how to get past the barricades? Gregory stopped to consider. He didn't want to use the main road, because that was where Henry and the Baron's strongest men would be stationed. The Baron's men were not trained soldiers, but lately Gregory had noticed his father hiring younger men and training them in combat techniques. Gregory had wondered about that. Now he knew why.

But most of the Baron's men were still ranchers, more used to wrestling difficult sheep or cows than fighting men. Gregory was a kind soul. Many of these men had helped raise him. After Lance's birth and the death of his wife, the Baron seemed to forget he had sons. It was men like Thomas who had looked out for Gregory, taught him to ride and hunt, and let him follow them around for companionship. He was a very lonely boy and they did their best to help him. Gregory appreciated and loved them and he didn't want to get them in trouble. His father would find out as soon as Gregory crossed the barricade line, so Gregory had to do it in a way that wouldn't cause collateral damage.

Gregory decided he wouldn't use the small trail he'd used before. He didn't know if Thomas was at that stop point, but he knew whoever was there, it would be only one man—easier for Gregory, but harder repercussions would fall on that one man, whoever he was. Gregory was quite certain that wherever he crossed, the guards would hesitate at least a *bit* before they raised their arrows to shoot at him.

Suddenly, it came to him.

He would cross on the secondary road where it crossed the Swift River. This checkpoint would have several guards, but not as many as the main checkpoint. The bridge crossing the river was only two horses wide, so the barricade to block it wouldn't be either very high or wide. And the best part was the road on each side of the bridge was winding—just like the river—so no one would see Gregory approaching until he was nearly there. Once across the bridge, the road turned so he would be out of sight—and out of arrow range—quickly.

Gregory thought, as he and Lightning started up again, *That's where I'll cross. Good thing I'm on you, Lightning. We've jumped so many obstacles together.*

It took them about a half hour to reach the barricade at Swift River. Gregory wished he could check it out first, but there was no way to see it without being seen. Gregory took a deep breath, gave Lightning an encouraging kick, and the two raced for the barricade, Gregory bent low over Lightning's neck.

As soon as Gregory had made the turn, and the barricade and bridge were in sight, he and Lightning put on speed. There were three guards. They looked up at the sound of the hooves, saw it was Gregory, and waved. They indicated that he should stop. Gregory was nearly on top of them before they realized he had no intention of stopping. They raised their bows just as Gregory and Lightning leapt over the barrier and thundered onto the bridge. Two of the three guards were men who had played with Gregory when he was a boy, but the third was one of the new men his father had hired. That guard was quicker off the mark and let an arrow loose.

Gregory felt a burning in his right shoulder, but he kept going. He was afraid that the next arrow would be aimed at Lightning, but before the guard could nock another, they were around the bend and out of sight. The pain in his shoulder throbbed, but he didn't stop. It wouldn't take long to get to Havenshold. He needed to let Clotilda and the others know what his father was planning. Lightning kept up a good pace. Thankfully, the horse knew the way, because Gregory started to lose consciousness from loss of blood.

As Lightning came galloping into the main courtyard at Havenshold, shouts were raised to stop. Lightning got to the edge of the courtyard and the riders could see that Gregory was slumped, unconscious, on Lightning's neck. Sylvester was the first on the scene. He gently lifted Gregory down. He motioned to a couple other workers to help him carry Gregory to the infirmary. A nurse came running over as soon as she saw them.

"Put him over here, *gently*," Nurse Beatrice said. "On his stomach. Sylvester, I know you've helped bandage dragons. This isn't so very different. Grab those bandages over there and the instruments in that tray. Hurry. I need to stop the bleeding."

Sylvester moved very fast. Beatrice couldn't have had a better assistant. Beatrice looked the wound over. "I'm going to have to snap the arrow off about two inches above the entry point, and then we'll have to cut an opening to get the arrow head out. I don't dare pull it, as I don't know if it's barbed."

"Right," said Sylvester. "I can cut the arrow and I'll get a mouth guard into Gregory's mouth so that if he starts regaining consciousness he won't bite his tongue in half."

As soon as Sylvester cut the arrow and got the mouth guard into Gregory's mouth, Beatrice took a scalpel and made a quick incision. "We're in luck—" she sighed, "—it's just a regular arrow."

"That's good," said Sylvester as he held Gregory still. The arrow was quickly removed, the antibiotic powder sprinkled in, the wound stitched and bandaged, and a sling fitted for him. "He's going to be very stiff and very sore, isn't he?" asked Sylvester.

"He sure is. If the Baron's insanity continues, this won't be the worst we have to deal with," answered Beatrice. "Let's get him into bed."

Just as they were trying to make Gregory comfortable, Emily came racing in. "I heard Gregory was shot. Is he OK? Where is he?"

Nurse Beatrice laughed. "Yes, Miss Emily. He's over here and he's doing fine. Took an arrow in his right shoulder, but Sylvester and I got it out and all stitched up. He'll be right as rain. I'd expect he'll be waking up pretty soon. He won't be very comfortable for a few days, but he'll heal just fine."

Emily said, "I was so worried!" Emily walked over to Gregory's bedside and looked down at him.

Gregory groaned and opened his eyes. He kept blinking, as if to get his eyes to focus. After a minute or so, he looked right at Emily and smiled.

"Hey, you don't have to do night patrol over the castle anymore," Gregory said with a laugh and a wince. "Thought I'd come here and save you the trouble."

"You idiot," answered Emily and smiled. *He'll be just fine,* she thought.

— 15 —

PRAGON RIDERS RESPOND

Nurse Beatrice started to chase Emily and Sylvester out of the infirmary, because Gregory needed to rest, but Gregory stopped her. "I have information that *must* be given to Clotilda right away. That's why I *jumped my father's barricade* and got *shot* to get here," said Gregory.

"You need *rest,*" said Beatrice firmly.

Emily said, "I'll get Clotilda." Both Emily and Sylvester left the infirmary.

Beatrice mixed up a pain and sleeping draught for Gregory. "I won't drink that *until* I speak with Clotilda," said Gregory. Thankfully, before another battle could break out, Clotilda and Emily returned.

Clotilda took a quick look at Gregory, saw that he wasn't in any real danger, nodded to Beatrice, and said, "OK, why are you giving Beatrice such a hard time?" She smiled.

Gregory tried to sit up, but only groaned and fell back against his pillows. "I have news," he said as pain clouded his eyes.

Clotilda noted his pain and said, "I'll hear a brief—and I do mean *brief*—report. Just the highlights. Tomorrow, after one of

Beatrice's wonderful healing draughts, you'll be in much better shape to fill in the details. You lost a lot of blood."

"I know." Gregory moaned. "My father's made an alliance... with King Stefan of Sanwight. King Stefan has...promised his oldest daughter, Priscilla, to...marry me...to unite the kingdoms."

"What?" said Clotilda and Emily in unison.

Emily suddenly realized that she didn't want to see Gregory marrying anyone...unless it was her.

Gregory continued, "I mentioned to my father that it... it should be Prince Rupert not...me, but my father just said that maybe King Jacob wouldn't always be...King and even so maybe Rupert would not be succeeding him. This was as close as my father got to declaring...declaring he was going to take over the throne of Draconia...I knew you needed to know this right away. If he's allied with King...Stefan, then he'll be getting armed forces from there in *addition* to his own men...Most of my father's men are not soldiers. If they were—" he took a deep breath, "—I wouldn't have gotten through the barricade at Swift River."

"You were lucky," answered Clotilda. "Very lucky. All right, any other details will have to wait 'til morning. I don't want to end up with Beatrice tackling us. Drink up your potion and we'll call a meeting for morning."

"OK," said Gregory, not entirely reluctantly. Now that he was here and had delivered his message, he wanted nothing more than to fall asleep and be out of pain. He quickly downed the foul-tasting potion and was asleep before the others left the room.

Clotilda had a quick word with Beatrice. "Call me if there are *any* changes. Not only has Gregory risked his life to bring us this news, but he's also the heir to the most powerful baron in the land."

"Don't worry," answered Beatrice. "I'll look after him as if he were one of us, which—" she looked slyly at Emily, "—he may soon be."

Emily blushed the deepest crimson and turned away. Clotilda smiled.

The dragon riders met in the assembly hall the next morning. Emily, seated beside Clotilda, watched as the other riders entered. Sylvester was standing at Gregory's side, ready to fetch anything he might need. Gregory looked very pale, but determined. He wasn't supposed to be out of the infirmary, but no one was going to keep him there.

Clotilda called the meeting to order. "Gregory has risked his *life* to break the barricade and bring us new information." She related the news of Gregory's impending betrothal to Priscilla. After the resultant hubbub died down, Clotilda continued. "I think it's safe to say that Baron Geldsmith is *determined* to become the next King of Draconia, and that he's going to be getting help from King Stefan *and* the Sanwight nobles. This greatly increases the threat to Draconia. While most of the Baron's men are not trained *fighters,* and none of them are *soldiers,* that is not true for Sanwight. They have an unusually large army and they pose a very real threat."

Anne said, "When Joseph and I were in Sanwight, Benjamin told us about the disharmony and unrest becoming worse by the day. On the one hand, there are a lot of fishermen who are trying to get rid of the ban on fishing nets—they want more money and they don't care about the dolphins' safety. Just as we must fight discrimination against dragons here, the dolphins and their riders are hated by many in Sanwight. They think that the dolphin riders are getting benefits without having to work, because the work of the dolphins and their riders isn't immediately apparent. The long lasting peace isn't attributed to them.

The fishermen also claim that it's *unnatural* for the dolphins to breathe air. They say they're mutations and should be outlawed."

Joseph said, "Benjamin was *sure* that it was Gregory's father who was spreading and inflaming the racial hatred in Sanwight, just as he is here in Draconia. All these younger sons are making careers in the army, careers which are nothing more than an excuse for drinking and gambling. The businessmen are baulking at paying for an army of such proportions when the country is at peace. I suspect the Baron wouldn't have to work hard at all to get King Stefan to agree to sending his army into Draconia. Once that happens, between them, they could get rid of dragons and dolphins and make everyone happy."

Clotilda said, "And with the upcoming betrothal announcement, sorry Gregory—" she added as she saw him wince, "—I think that their timetable for invasion is probably *close*. So, how do we defend Draconia *and* the King? Ideas?" She looked first at Emily to be sure she was ready to take down any ideas and then turned to the group at large.

Hans spoke first. "I've been thinking about this and picking some of the brains around here," he said with a smile. "We think that if we had about thirteen dragons that we could defend the pass between Draconia and Sanwight. It wouldn't be easy, but the pass is extremely narrow."

"That's very true," answered Clotilda. "But it's also very *dangerous*. You've worked out the numbers, so you're in charge. Find your volunteers, gather your supplies, and let me know when you're ready to head out."

"Right," said Hans. "We won't let Draconia down. I promise."

"Try to stay *alive*," said Clotilda. She turned to the congregation. "What else can we do?"

"Our people here have been very good and very loyal, but we're running low on supplies," said William. "Thunder and I went out last night. The supply wagons that have been turned back are just sitting in the valley below us, right off the main road. I would like to volunteer to try to get some of those supplies up here. We'll need them *very* soon."

"I'm sure they're being guarded," said Clotilda. "What's your plan?"

William's expression was sheepish and he hesitated, looking down at his feet before beginning. "Dragons can lift more than twice their body weight, even with a rider on them, so I thought if I could get someone to go with me, between us, our dragons ought to be able to lift a couple wagons by the horse-harnesses."

There was a loud outburst of laughter. William ducked his head. When the laughter quieted, Clotilda said, "I hope the back end of the wagon is secured or else everything will fall out." She looked at William with kind eyes.

Jake interrupted the laughter that still lingered. "William has a *good* plan, but he needs *more* help. If we had two dragons on *each* wagon, we could bring them into the air fairly level. That way we wouldn't lose much of anything. With four dragons, we'd be better protected from any guards. Even the most *ruthless* guard can be intimidated by a little fire."

"What do you think, William?" asked Clotilda.

Emily thought *It is amazing to watch Clotilda lead. She is able to encourage everyone and give everyone the space, encouragement, and time to put forth ideas.*

"I think it's great," replied William, blushing. "And, if Jake's willing, I'd rather he be in command. He has a lot more experience than I do."

"If you're sure...I'd be happy to follow *you,* William," replied Jake, smiling and giving a slight bow.

Emily noticed that William blushed at this comment.

"Thanks, Jake, but I trust you." He faced Clotilda again. "When I was thinking about this, Joseph and Anne said they wanted to help out. Are you two still game?" asked William.

They both nodded.

"All right," said Clotilda. "Go for it tonight. Let's see if we can't get our people something to *lift* their spirits." She chuckled at her pun. "I've been astonished and *greatly* touched by the fact that no one has decided to leave. These are people who *love* our dragons. They deserve a surprise. This meeting is over. Everyone has a lot to do."

"Wait!" shouted Gregory, and everyone turned to look. "I was wondering, should we try to reach the King and let him know what's happening? Maybe he'll let us know what the Baron's hold is over him."

"I thought of that also," answered Clotilda. "Honestly, I don't think we could get a dragon and rider anywhere near him."

"True, but *I* could get to him, I'm sure," answered Gregory.

"What?" Emily nearly shouted. "You nearly got yourself *killed* yesterday!"

"That was a fluke. Besides, only a person on horseback could make it to the Capitol, and King Jacob knows and trusts me. I'm feeling much better and another night with more of Beatrice's potion should have me nearly good as new," replied Gregory.

"Emily, he's right." Clotilda looked at Gregroy. "But you *can't* go alone and that is final."

"I'll go with him," answered Sylvester right away. "It's our fathers that are causing this uproar, we should try and make amends."

"All right," conceded Clotilda. "But I also want Emily in the group. She can keep in touch with Esmeralda and through her, with us. You three work up a plan by the morning. If it looks viable, and if you really are *that* much better, Gregory, then the three of you may set out just after dawn."

The group disbanded. Sylvester helped Gregory back to the infirmary. As soon as he had Gregory safely in bed he said, "I've found a secret path through the mountains, really *close* to that small hunting path you used the last time you went home. I think I could get us through that way and we could also return unnoticed. You wouldn't even have to take another arrow."

Gregory was starting to nod off, but he laughed and answered, "That sounds good. Thanks for volunteering to come with me. There's no one I'd rather have covering my back. Let me get a quick nap. This evening we'll find Emily and plan in earnest."

Sylvester said, "Rest up. You'll need your strength!"

Gregory was already asleep. Sylvester smiled and headed out to do his work.

— 16 —

MEETING WITH THE KING

During the night, as Gregory slept with Beatrice's medicine coursing through his body, Jake and Harmony led the raiding party to capture a couple supply wagons.

There were four riders and dragons—Jake and Harmony with William and Thunder for one wagon, and Anne and Samantha and Joseph and Spruce for the other. They took off in the darkest part of the night and swooped down on the wagons before the guards even knew they were there.

Jake instructed Anne and Joseph to move in first. That wagon was airborne before the guards could fire.

Jake and William weren't so lucky. William and Thunder took the front of the wagon while Jack and Harmony took the rear. By now the guards were *thinking* and one of them decided to fire flaming arrows. Just as they were airborne, Harmony was hit with a flaming arrow in her left wing. She howled with pain and shot fire back at the guards, burning one badly, but Jake helped her stay focused. He monitored her pain through their bond, and even took some of the pain into himself. William had to assist Thunder to compensate for the fact that Harmony only had one wing.

The motley group flew at a very wonky angle back to the Havenshold courtyard. They ended up crashing down abruptly and the wagon broke apart. The supplies were mostly intact.

All anyone cared about was Harmony, whose cries of pain woke most of Havenshold. Sylvester came racing out with his dragon medic kit. He and Jake set to work, spreading pain-numbing medicine over the burned wing while sending calming, loving thoughts to Harmony.

Clotilda and Matilda came out. Matilda used her telepathic power to keep Harmony still and relatively pain-free until the medicines took over. Emily and Esmeralda leant their assistance as well.

Once they were done with all the first aid, Jake took Harmony to their cave. He promised he'd let them know if there was anything more that could be done. Emily and Esmeralda offered to bring them food and water and to take over Jake's chores until Harmony was well. Everyone was relieved to learn that Harmony's injuries would heal. The arrow had barely caught the outer edge of her wing and fortunately the fire hadn't spread. The arrow had just been lit by the campfire, without fuel, and so it had burned out quickly.

As Jake and Harmony were leaving, Clotilda said, "We need to be *alert* for this in the future. The Baron's men are learning that their arrows are not very effective against us. I would expect that tonight's episode will only encourage them to use *real* flaming arrows in the future. We must think of ways we can protect ourselves—and more importantly our *dragons*—from such tactics. Now, back to bed everyone. Tomorrow will be here soon."

The next morning dawned cold and clear.

Clotilda met with Emily, Gregory, and Sylvester, and learned that Sylvester had discovered a secret break in the mountain rocks—thanks to a stray sheep he had rescued a month ago—which would allow them to leave, and hopefully return, to Havenshold without having to cross a barricade. An added benefit was that the route was *much* shorter than going by the main road.

Clotilda also received a report from Beatrice that Gregory was fit for duty if he kept his arm free from strain. Therefore, Clotilda agreed to having Emily, Gregory, and Sylvester try to meet with King Jacob.

"Best of luck," she said as she agreed to their plan. "Please be back by nightfall, as tonight the thirteen dragon riders are heading out to start defending the pass. As soon as that's known, *all* the Baron's defenses will be tightened. I don't want you trapped on the wrong side."

"We'll be back tonight," said Gregory. "It is much faster to ride to the Capitol than to hike there."

Emily, Gregory, and Sylvester mounted their horses and headed out. They were lucky that Sylvester had trained a few horses to stay calm around dragons. He had a way with creatures, dragons, and people alike that was very soothing. Gregory saw Esmeralda high above them and waved back at her. He sent her thanks for being nearby.

Sylvester led the way out of Havenshold. Just before they would reach the road to the Swift River bridge, Sylvester branched off to the left.

"Where are we going?" asked Gregory. "I've been down this road before. Isn't it a dead end?"

"That's what I always thought," replied Sylvester, "until one day when I was hunting a lost sheep. I found tracks going right up to the end, and then darned if they didn't disappear around this rock here. You can't see the opening except from this *one* spot," said Sylvester as he led them around what had always *seemed* to be a dead end that stopped at a boulder.

As soon as they were around the boulder, Gregory saw the narrow opening, just big enough for a horse to squeeze through. Sylvester continued, "I just assumed it was a small cavern where the sheep had gotten herself trapped, but as you'll see, it opens out to a small path that works its way down the mountain and comes out onto the main road to the Capitol on the *other* side of the blockade."

"Wonderful!" said Emily. "Let's go."

They went through the crack—first Sylvester, then Emily, and finally Gregory. The horses were not thrilled with the narrow confines, and the rider's boots rubbed the side of the opening, but soon they were through. After that, it was an easy ride through deserted forests. A few hours of swift riding later they came out, just as Sylvester had said, onto the main road *very* close to the Capitol.

Emily said, "I sure wish I'd known about this route when we had to do our forced march to the capitol." Esmeralda chuckled from high above them and both Gregory and Sylvester heard her. It made them all feel lighter in spirit.

"Not only did we get past the barricade, but we cut *miles* off our journey," said Gregory. "Let's get to the Palace and find King Jacob."

As the three rode into the Capitol, they noticed that everyone was acting strangely. No one was ambling or browsing the shop windows. Everyone was moving with purpose, hurrying along to get their errands done. Gregory noticed a lot of new faces as well—faces of men like the thugs he'd seen his father with at the hatching.

"We need to be careful," said Gregory, quietly. "Something isn't right here."

Emily and Sylvester agreed. They walked directly toward the Palace as if they had every right to be there. As they approached the Palace steps, Sylvester whispered, "Don't look, but we're being followed by three unsavory-looking characters. They're right behind us."

"I noticed them too. What do you say that we teach them a lesson?" answered Gregory.

Sylvester smiled. "What did you have in mind?"

Gregory, Emily, and Sylvester whispered for a few moments and then moved forward. They entered the main gates of the Palace, and dismounted, hitching their horses to the rail just inside the gates.

Gregory and Emily started to turn left when Sylvester called out, "You won't need me and I'm hungry. Is it all right if I stop by the kitchens? I'll meet you back at the horses later."

"Ok," replied Gregory as he continued on with Emily through the left side of the circular outer courtyard. The three men consulted for a minute and then appeared to decide that they needed to follow Gregory and Emily.

Emily and Gregory continued walking to the northeast corner, and then they began to argue.

"It's this way!" Emily said.

"No, we've gone too far."

"I'm sure it is this way."

"Well it isn't." Gregory swore under his breathe. He and Emily turned around and headed back toward their followers.

Emily saw the three thugs, but pretended they were palace staff. She smiled sweetly and said, "Where is the main entrance? We seemed to have gotten turned around."

The three men seemed unsure of their actions and started to answer, only to find that Sylvester was behind them and they were trapped with Emily and Gregory on one side and Sylvester on the other.

The leader of the group said, "You aren't supposed to be here. No visitors allowed in the palace."

"On whose orders?" asked Gregory

"Baron Geldsmith," replied the leader.

"Well," continued Gregory in a mild tone. "We need to see King Jacob, so please step out of our way."

"Didn't you hear me?" snarled the leader. *"No visitors."*

At that point, Sylvester swung his fist right into the stomach of the thug closest to him and Gregory grabbed the leader by the wrist and flipped him over his shoulder. As the third man was deciding what to do, Emily tripped him and Sylvester sent a neat upper cut to his chin. Down he went.

Sylvester had gotten rope when he appeared to go off to the kitchens. They tied up the thugs, slung them over a low wall into a drainage ditch, and then proceeded to enter the main door of the Palace.

They saw King Jacob's secretary, Bernard, sitting at a desk in the corner of a large room. They approached him and requested an audience with the King.

Bernard looked *very* nervous. "I'm n-n-not allowed to set up appointments for the K-K-King anymore," he stuttered. "The Baron has left a couple men stationed here...to h-h-help the King with such d-d-details."

"Has he now?" Gregory said, "Well, that's *just* like my father, *ever so helpful,* I'm sure. Do you know where the King is?"

"He's finishing lunch with the Queen," replied Bernard. "They're in their private dining room, but there are guards stationed outside in the hall."

"Very inconvenient," said Gregory. "We have important news that the King needs to hear. Any ideas on how we might arrange a meeting?"

Bernard smiled, a bit calmer now. He'd always been kind to Gregory. Bernard was fiercely loyal to King Jacob. He'd been the King's personal secretary for over thirty years. Gregory knew he could trust him.

"Well," said Bernard very softly, "there's *another* way into the dining room that none of the guards knows about. See that tapestry over there on the wall? The one with the fountain in the middle?" They nodded. "Right behind it is a small door. I'm the only one with the key. The door leads to a long corridor. The other end of the corridor opens into the dining room behind another tapestry, also with a fountain in the middle.

"Here's the key," he said as he slid a piece of paper toward Gregory. Gregory lifted the corner slightly and quickly grabbed the key. Bernard then said more loudly and with a stern expression, "I'm sorry, as I said, the King is seeing *no one* today."

"Guess we've had a long ride for nothing. We'll head out," said Gregory.

He, Emily, and Sylvester walked to the other side of the room and slipped quickly and quietly behind the tapestry just as Bernard was yelling at someone on the other side of the room—a distraction.

It was exactly as Bernard had said. The key opened the door, and they were quickly through, locking the door behind them from the other side. They hurried down the long corridor, unlocked the door at the other end, and slipped through.

They heard King Jacob speaking to the crying Queen. "It *will* be all right," said King Jacob. "If I just do everything Baron Geldsmith wants, we'll soon have Rupert back. He *promised.*" At this moment, Gregory, Emily, and Sylvester stepped from behind the tapestry and the King saw them. "Gregory! What are you doing here?"

"Trying to help you, sire," replied Gregory as the three of them knelt.

"I don't understand," said the King. "How did you know about that passage? Your father will be *furious* if he gets wind of this. He's kidnapped our Rupert. I can't take any chances with my son's life. Get out, quickly!"

Gregory spoke quietly and quickly. "There are things you *need to know,* sire, and there's information *we* also need. We can *stop* my father, but only if we work together. Clotilda sent us. Do you know Emily? She is in training with Clotilda. Sylvester's father is my father's foreman. We had no idea that Rupert's life was in jeopardy. When was he kidnapped?"

Queen Marigold sobbed. "Right after the Dragon Riders' Graduation. That was the last happy day we had!"

"I'm so very sorry, your majesty. I'm horrified that my father is behind all this," said Gregory, "but you don't have to do this alone. We'll help get Rupert back safely, I promise."

Gregory quickly told the King and Queen all that was transpiring—how his father was trying to form an allegiance with King Stefan to take over the throne, even arranging a betrothal for him with Priscilla.

"We had no idea that the Baron's plans were so far-reaching," said King Jacob. "I just thought he was letting his hatred of dragons drive him. Once the dragons were gone I was sure he would be satisfied. I should have known better."

"No," said Gregory. "My father hates the dragons because he was never chosen, and neither were his sons. He hates any kind of power he can't wield. He'd be absolutely furious if he knew that I begged the dragons not to pick me."

King Jacob looked up, startled. "You can talk with dragons? How is that possible? I miss my beautiful Henrietta so much, every single day, but she only spoke to me. I thought that was how it was."

Emily spoke up. "We're learning a great deal about telepathy and how the dragons communicate, sire. Once this hideous nightmare is over, we'd be honored to share some of our research. But for now, we have to stop the Baron. One reason

Clotilda sent me is that I can keep in contact with my dragon, Esmeralda, who is stationed about half way between your palace and Havenshold. That way, by relaying messages, Clotilda and Matilda can advise us and stay informed."

"You're right. I've been a fool to think that I had to do this by myself. My personal guard has stayed loyal to me, I know, which is why your father has replaced most of them in the Palace. But Bernard—it was Bernard who got you in here, wasn't it?"

Gregory nodded.

"Bernard," the King continued, "knows where they're hiding, and I can have them rallied and sent out of the city to the pass to help your riders. It'll probably take them three days to get there. Can you show me on my map where your secret road is, Sylvester? That way the Palace guard—around fifty men—can reach the pass without the Baron knowing. I think that would be safest for Rupert."

As Sylvester pointed to the path's location, Gregory continued, "Your guards will be a *huge* help."

The King said, "I know they've been disappointed in the way I caved under the Baron, but any who have children will understand...although for a King, it isn't very noble. I was horrified to hear that the Baron had blockaded Havenshold. That wasn't on my orders. I was hoping that agreeing to banishment would be enough and that we could sort this out."

"We understand," replied Emily. "And don't worry about the blockade. We managed to get supplies through last night—although one dragon, Harmony, got her wing badly burned. She'll be all right. The main thing is to get the pass protected so that Sanwight troops *can't* get through. We need to get out of here and back to Havenshold to help." The King nodded.

"By the way," said Gregory, "We dumped a couple thugs over the low north wall into the ravine. Your city isn't a happy one."

King Jacob nodded. "I know. I need to take steps, *soon*, before the Baron's thugs do real damage. Thank you, all. I don't think you should go out the way you came in. Give me Bernard's key. There's another passage behind that tapestry over there. It's never locked. It comes out on the north side not too far from where you tied up your horses. You should be able to make your way home from there. Thank you for letting us know we aren't alone."

They did as the King suggested and were on their way with no further problems. No one followed them as they left the Capitol, and by nightfall they were back at Havenshold to give Clotilda a full report.

— 17 —

PASS DEFENSES BEGUN

After Emily, Gregory, and Sylvester reported to Clotilda, the news that Rupert had been kidnapped spread quickly. The next morning, everyone met to discuss plans of action.

As always, Clotilda, with Emily at her side, began the meeting. She looked around the room at Gregory and her dragon riders. "Hans, do you have your thirteen volunteers for defending the pass?"

"Yes," replied Hans. "In fact I got a lot more. Here's the list." Hans handed a sheet of paper to Clotilda.

Clotilda looked over the list and replied, "It is great to see so many volunteers, but I think thirteen is the right number. Any more and we'll be more of a danger to ourselves than the enemy. Emily and Esmeralda will be your second in command so Emily can help keep us informed while also gaining command experience." She took a pen and marked her choices. "Here's your group," said Clotilda, handing the paper back to Hans. "Now get whatever supplies you need. Take enough for at *least* a week. As soon as it's dark, head up to the pass. Matilda can communicate with Fire Dancer and Esmeralda, so keep me abreast of any new developments."

"Right you are," answered Hans.

"Next we need to address the issue of Prince Rupert's kidnapping," said Clotilda. "I'm nearly positive that he isn't being held in Draconia—unless he is hidden in the Baron's lands—or someone would have leaked the news."

Gregory's hand shot up. "I know the Prince isn't at our castle, so my guess would be that my father has him in Sanwight, at his house there. It's large enough to hide him, and it's being guarded. We need to get to him quickly. He's only twelve."

"That's a reasonable guess," said Clotilda. "Anne, Joseph— may I ask you two to try to get in contact with Benjamin again and see if you can learn more?"

Anne smiled broadly. Joseph stood up straighter. "We thought we'd need Benjamin again, so we've set up a rendezvous spot just on the other side of the pass. We'll tag along with Hans's group and move on from there, if that's OK."

"Yes," answered Clotilda, "but be careful, and please don't take any unnecessary chances with either yourselves *or* Rupert. Send a report to Matilda whenever you learn anything."

"Will do," replied Joseph. The two headed out of the room to catch up with Hans.

"Now, William, how are Jake and Harmony doing?" asked Clotilda.

"They're doing great," replied William, quietly. His normally well-groomed appearance was missing. His large brown eyes had dark circles under them and his brown hair was standing up in the back, indicating that he hadn't gotten much sleep. "She's regenerating skin pretty fast. The pain is pretty much gone and Jake figures they can try short flights by tonight."

"Wonderful," said Clotilda. The room echoed with loud cheering from the other riders. When the noise died down, Clotilda asked about the success of the raid.

"We were really lucky," said William. "We had to grab the easiest wagons we could, but the two we snatched were full of fresh produce and flour. Since those were the items we were lowest on, the commissary clerk thinks that the entire population of Havenshold will be well fed and stocked for at *least* two weeks if we plan carefully."

"Excellent!" said Clotilda "Please give your inventory list to Emily."

William blushed and nodded.

Clotilda said, "Those of you who are remaining , for the moment at least, I want you to think about defensive measures we can take *here* to protect our people in case the army breaks through at the pass. It would be good if we could think of a way to defend against flaming arrows, too."

William said, "As a first measure, please be sure *all* riders are carrying sandbags. Harmony was lucky—if you're ever lucky being struck by a flaming arrow—because the arrow had not been soaked in any incendiary materials. If the rider has sand handy, then even a *fierce* fire could be smothered relatively quickly. It's better than nothing. Also, I'm going to try to come up with a flame-retardant spray we can spray the wings with. So far I haven't gotten anything that works very well."

"Thanks, William," answered Clotilda. "I'll order that all riders carry sand. You're relieved of all other duties so you can concentrate on that flame retardant. That is your number one priority."

"Yes, Ma'am," said William. He ran out of the hall to get back to his lab.

"That's it for now," said Clotilda. "Everyone knows what they need to do. Good luck!"

Later that night, Hans, Emily, Anne, Joseph, and the other eleven riders mounted their dragons and headed out to the pass between Draconia and Sanwight. It took a couple hours, but they didn't run into any trouble and it didn't seem as if any of the Baron's men had spotted them. They were very glad that this entrance into Havenshold wasn't subject to a blockade. The Baron had requested that Sanwight not allow people to use that pass without special permission, but from the Draconian side it was clear of interference.

The pass itself was five miles long and varied in width. It wasn't wide enough for more than four soldiers abreast and in certain places it was only wide enough for one or two. The advancing army would be composed of foot soldiers, but there would also be the Baron and any of his nobles on horseback.

Most of the pass was too narrow for dragons to fly safely in, so the dragons would have to fly above, sending down bolts of fire. However, they would then also be within arrow range—the canyon walls only rose about ten feet above the path.

Hans called his riders together. "We'll make camp here at the top of the pass still inside Draconia. We don't want to start problems and be seen as an invasion into Sanwight. It's *imperative* that we hold the army here. If they're allowed to break through, there would be no way for a group as small as ours to stop them before they reached the Capitol."

Emily spoke for the other riders as second in command. "We won't give an inch. You tell us what to do, Hans, and we'll do it."

Hans smiled and his face softened. "Thanks, Emily...Do you have *any* idea how much trouble I'd be in if Mom and Dad knew I'd let you be part of this group?"

Emily smiled. "I'll make sure they know that you couldn't stop us. You need a purple dragon as leader, and we can't afford to have Matilda and Clotilda out on the front lines, so you're stuck with me. But don't worry, Esmeralda and I will be your second in command, and we'll be fine."

Hans smiled and turned to address the greater group. "The first thing we need to do is get Anne and Joseph safely through the pass and on to their meeting with Benjamin. So far, the

Baron hasn't left anyone here. He prefers to go to Sanwight using a tiny trail out of his estate, but thankfully that trail is too small and overgrown to march an army on it so the army will have to come this way. Anne, how far on the other side of the pass is your rendezvous spot?"

"Just a mile down the road on the Sanwight side. Benjamin promised to be there before dawn each day. If we go now, we should catch him," answered Anne.

"OK, sounds good. Go see what you can learn about Rupert," said Hans.

Anne and Joseph mounted their dragons and flew over the pass and out of sight, almost silently.

"As for the rest of us," said Hans, "I want each of you to explore this pass and learn *every square inch.* Figure out how to recognize from both the air and the ground where it widens and narrows. We may have to fight on foot with our dragons above us, although if the King's personal guard can get here before the army, we'll have fifty trained soldiers on foot, and we'll be above on our dragons. Gregory wasn't sure if the King's men would get here soon enough, so we'll play it by ear."

The dragons and riders spent the next morning scouting the pass. Some thought they should get rope to string across the path in places to trip the soldiers. Others thought about blockades. Some had found rocks they could hide behind and shoot from without being vulnerable to returning fire.

Hans told everyone to rest while he and Emily considered all the options. He was just getting ready to have Fire Dancer contact Matilda when he saw Anne and Joseph returning. They landed and came over to him.

"We know where Rupert is!" Anne burst out.

"Benjamin had men secretly watching the Baron's house in Sanwight," said Joseph. "One evening, as it was starting to get dark, they noticed a figure at the window at the very top of the house. The figure was waving frantically, but he was suddenly yanked away and the curtains were closed tight again. Benjamin's spy was *sure* it was a young boy—it has to be Rupert."

"Sounds like it," said Hans. "Does Benjamin know anything about the house?"

Anne replied, "Benjamin said that there are six men on a rotating duty when the Baron is out of the country, along with a housekeeper, but at night it appears that there are only three men on duty and everyone else is asleep. Rupert is being kept in a tiny room at the very top of the house."

"Benjamin thinks that his men can get Rupert out of there. They've been working on a plan. They want to free Rupert before the Baron comes on his next visit. They're set to mount the rescue tonight. If they succeed they'll bring Rupert to our rendezvous spot, and then Anne and I will fly him home to his parents," answered Joseph.

Anne continued, "I think it would be a good idea if one of us participated in the rescue. After all, Rupert has to be pretty scared—although that was very brave of him to wave from the window—and he doesn't know *anyone* from Sanwight. But he knows *us*. We met at the Dragon Rider Graduation."

"Good thought, Anne," answered Hans. "Joseph, you go with Benjamin and his men for the rescue, and then get back to the rendezvous to hand Rupert over to Anne and Samantha. Then, you and Spruce fly as close to them as you can for added protection."

Anne nodded. Joseph said, "We'd better get back to Benjamin and let him know. If all goes smoothly, Rupert should be back at the Palace by tomorrow."

"Fire Dancer can reach Samantha even when you're in Sanwight, so don't be foolish. If you need help, send for it. I know it would make a major diplomatic incident if we flew dragons into Sanwight, but they're holding the heir to our lands *against* his will. They may not know what the Baron is doing, but we have every *right* to rescue Rupert. Try to do this without involving Draconia, but Rupert's safety is the first priority," concluded Hans. Anne and Joseph headed out.

We'd better chat with Matilda and Clotilda, old girl, thought Hans affectionately to Fire Dancer. Soon, Clotilda had been apprised of the developments. She applauded their efforts, approved Hans's plans to defend the pass, and was overjoyed to hear that that dolphin riders were determined to rescue Rupert.

— 18 —

RESCUE AND DEFENSE

Hans couldn't stand around waiting. He was worried about Anne and Joseph, and since he knew nothing about the dolphin riders, also concerned that maybe the they weren't up to rescuing Rupert—but he had no better ideas and it wasn't his country. He just had to *trust* Benjamin. Benjamin and the dolphin riders were in as much danger as were the dragons and dragon riders. They would want to help. There was no telling when the Baron would return, so now that they knew where Rupert was, they had to act quickly. That didn't make Hans's job any easier. He was still stuck waiting. Rather than just worry, he rousted his riders from their well-earned afternoon siestas and presented his plan for the defense of the pass.

"Listen up," he said. "I've taken into account all your ideas. None of them is the perfect solution, but together I think they *will* work. First, there are some boulders above and below the pass. They're too big to be moved by men, but not too much for a couple of dragons. I want you to work in teams. We need major boulders placed in all the spots that are more than two soldiers wide. Each team should have two dragons and two riders."

It was very hard work. After several hours, Hans called a halt. "OK, let's stop for dinner. Nice work. We've moved nearly twenty boulders and I think we've improved the defensibility of this pass. They'll never be able to come through more than two at a time, so even though they'll have many more than us, those numbers can't be brought against us in force."

Emily asked, "Are we also going to string the ropes?"

"I've thought about that. I don't think the ropes will be very effective against slow moving foot soldiers—that strategy works much better on cavalry—but what about tying medium size rocks onto ropes that are fastened to the trees, and then cutting the ropes as the officers go by? It should knock them off their horses, which hopefully will be spooked," answered Hans.

Emily smiled. "I like that."

"We can refine all this over the next day or so. We need to keep look-outs posted so that we can see when the army starts advancing. We can see about three miles along the road into Sanwight, so we'll get plenty of warning. Hopefully, they won't have *any* idea what we're doing. Emily, please set up a watch roster," said Hans. "OK, now for the big news," continued Hans. "Anne and Joseph reported that Benjamin and his dolphin riders have *located* Prince Rupert. They're staging a rescue attempt tonight. If they're successful, then Anne and Joseph will be taking Prince Rupert back to his parents before morning."

The riders all cheered. When the cheers died down, Hans continued. "We need to be ready in case they need help. Samantha will call to Fire Dancer to keep us updated, and if needed, we'll invade to rescue our prince. Meanwhile, let's see if we can find more boulders to move in the remaining light." The dragon riders groaned. "After that, there'll be nothing for us to do but wait for news and dawn."

Anne and Joseph met up with Benjamin and he agreed to taking Joseph along. Anne was to wait with Samantha and Spruce as the rest set off for the Baron's house in Sanwight. If there were any problems, Joseph would tell Spruce, who would then tell Anne and Samantha. The lines of communication were open as Benjamin, Joseph, and nine other dolphin riders marched off, leaving Anne to wait.

Benjamin and his men arrived near the Baron's house and met up with their spy.

"All quiet," the spy reported. "They've just finished cleaning up after dinner. I think the boy's in bed already."

Benjamin nodded. He and his men settled down to wait.

Joseph thought, *Does campaigning always require so much waiting?*

When it was completely dark with only the stars above, Benjamin signaled his men to move out. The plan was to have Joseph stay with Benjamin so that they would be the ones to storm the top bedroom first. Rupert would recognize Joseph.

The men circled the house. One of them knocked on the back door. When a man answered, Benjamin grabbed his arm, jerked him outside, and flipped him onto the ground—knocking him out before they tied him up. They all quickly entered the house. They found the housekeeper asleep and bolted her door so that she couldn't get out if she woke. The other two guards were dispatched without fuss. First, Benjamin approached the one at the bottom of the stairs, holding out his hand toward him. The guard, taken by surprise, acted instinctively to the handshake gesture. Before he could do anything else, Benjamin had grabbed him by the wrist and flipped him over onto the floor where one of his men slapped tape across his face and tied him up. The other guard, at the top of the stairs, made the mistake of heading down to see what the noise was all about. He was dispatched by a blow to the back of his neck just as he came around the corner of the hall.

With the guards taken care of, Benjamin and Joseph entered the bedroom. Joseph rushed over to Rupert's bed and gently woke him with a hand on his shoulder. "Rupert, we're here to rescue you," said Joseph.

"Who are you?" started Rupert, but then he said, "Hey, I know you—you just graduated as a dragon rider!"

"Yes, Prince Rupert," replied Joseph. "I'm Joseph, and I'm here with these fine dolphin riders to get you out of here and *back* to your parents. Now come on, we have to hurry. Climb on my back and hold on tight."

Soon, they were on their way out of the town. So far, no alarm had been raised. They felt lucky, but they ran nonetheless all the way to the rendezvous spot. Joseph handed Rupert up to Anne, who was already mounted on Samantha. He jumped onto Spruce.

"Do I get to ride a dragon?" asked Prince Rupert, his eyes wide in his small, round face.

"You sure do. Her name's Samantha," answered Anne.

"Cool," replied Prince Rupert.

Yes, Prince, it will be cool. Cold even. Samantha chuckled.

"I heard her! I heard her!" shouted Prince Rupert.

Anne smiled, "Yes, she was making a bit of a joke, but she's right. This will be a cold ride. I need you to snuggle inside my cloak so it keeps us both warm."

"Thank you, Benjamin! And thank your men for us!" shouted Joseph.

Rupert's small voice rang out from inside Anne's cloak. "Thank you, dolphin riders, for saving me!"

Benjamin and his riders waved. "We'll be in touch. I think Horace finally spoke to Samantha. When the need is urgent and you are nearby, it seems to work."

Anne, Joseph, and Prince Rupert took to the skies. As they flew over the pass, their fellow dragons and riders cheered them on. By dawn they were flying high over the Palace.

"This could be tricky," said Joseph. "We're supposed to be banished. I have no desire to get this close and then get shot down."

Prince Rupert began shouting, "Mommy, Daddy, I'm home! Where are you?"

The guards looked up and saw the two dragons. They began drawing their bows, but by now Prince Rupert's little voice could be clearly heard.

"Put those bows down! These dragons have rescued me! This is your prince and I *command* you!" he said in his loudest voice, though it shook.

It didn't look as if the Baron's lackey's were about to take orders from a twelve-year-old boy, even if he was heir to the throne, so both Samantha and Spruce started to bellow, which woke up the entire Palace.

The King stuck his head out of his window to see what the ruckus was all about and saw his son riding on a dragon—waving and cheering. The King called to the guards in the courtyard, "Put your weapons down. I don't care what orders you have from the Baron, you'll be taking *my* orders from now on!"

The guards dropped their weapons and ran out of the Palace, since at the moment there was no one left to stop them. They needed to report right away if they stood any chance of living to see another dawn.

Samantha and Spruce landed in the large open courtyard just as King Jacob and Queen Marigold came running out in their nightdresses, both sobbing hysterically. "Rupert, Rupert! You're back! Are you OK?" Queen Marigold asked through her tears.

It took awhile to sort everything out, but eventually the King and Queen learned what had happened and where Rupert had been held. Rupert said he hadn't been beaten, just threatened. He told how he'd tried to wave out the window, but wasn't sure if anyone had seen him.

Joseph let him know that his actions had indeed been seen and had resulted in tonight's rescue. Joseph and Anne also made sure that the King and Queen knew that it was Benjamin and the dolphin riders who had really pulled off the rescue.

Joseph and Anne got back on their dragons and headed off to Havenshold. The reunited family went back into the Palace as a new dawn was breaking.

— 19 —

BARON REACTS

The Baron was awakened by loud pounding on his bedroom door at 6:00 a.m. He climbed out of bed to answer it.

Henry came in shouting. "The dragon riders rescued Rupert! He's back with his parents at the Palace."

"Damn!" said the Baron. "How did that happen? I thought he was well-guarded."

"The dolphin riders were worried by both your actions and the fishermen's pleas to lift the ban on fishing nets. They performed the rescue. They got him to the dragon riders at the border. The King was very angry. We won't get him to turn on the dragons again," said Henry.

The Baron said, "Go get my sons. We'll leave for Sanwight immediately. The date for the invasion must be moved up to as soon as possible. We ride now!"

Henry quickly returned. "Gregory's gone. Lance says he saw him ride out of here yesterday," reported Henry.

"I was afraid of that," said the Baron. "He took the betrothal news much too calmly. He's turned on us. That means that most of our plans are known. We will have to move very quickly. What about Lance?"

Lance walked in. "Father, I'm *not* going to be part of any coup to overthrow King Jacob. I want to be a good son and honor your wishes, but this is isn't right. I won't give you away or betray you—as Gregory has—but I also *won't* assist you. I ask to be allowed to stay here and look after your lands and livestock, to run things in your absence. If I stay, then you can take Henry, who will be much more use to you. I love you, Father, but *this is wrong.* I wish you could see that. If Mother were alive, I know she'd stop you."

"Well, she isn't, damn it! She died giving birth to *you,* you ungrateful wretch! Fine, stay if you want. I don't want any *cowards* traveling with me. Come on, Henry. Round up as many of our men as you can. Lance, you can deal with things here. On your own." The Baron snarled.

"I will, Father. I'll keep everything safe," replied Lance, with eyes that looked wet, as he left.

The Baron said, "There isn't much point to the blockades now. The war will be decided before Havenshold runs out of supplies after their raid, so get all the men from the blockades and let's march for Sanwight. You can leave a skeleton crew behind of the old hands, but bring everyone else. We march in an hour. Why am I plagued with such *ungrateful* sons? Don't they know I'm *doing this for them?*"

Within the hour, the Baron and roughly fifty men were ready to ride. They took the back trail to Sanwight. It was treacherous and they had to go slowly, single file, but they were not observed. Soon they were across the border and heading for the Baron's home in Sanwight. They arrived shortly after noon. As soon as the Baron had gotten lunch, he sent for the Sanwight rebel nobles.

The nobles were most distressed. They'd heard about Rupert's kidnapping and subsequent rescue.

Terence asked, "Why did you kidnap an *innocent* child?"

The Baron laughed. "How else did you think I could convince King Jacob to turn on the dragons? We had to have a *strong* hold over him. The child wasn't harmed. We just kept him away from his parents, but *someone* found out. It doesn't matter now. He's safe with his Mommy and Daddy, but it means that we need to march on Draconia *as soon as possible.* How long will it take you to get your troops up to the pass?"

Terence blurted, "Now, hold on. We also hear that Gregory has *refused* King Stefan's offer of Priscilla's hand in marriage. What assurances do we have that once we put you on Draconia's throne, you'll honor your alliance with us?"

"Oh, that," said the Baron dismissively with a wave of his hand. "Don't worry. I wasn't keen on Gregory having her anyway. She'll make a perfect bride for me. That way, she'll become queen right away, rather than after I die. It'll be an even *stronger* bond. The King should be happy."

Terence nodded. "In that case," said Terence, "I'll get my commanders to assemble the troops and we'll start marching for the border pass. We can camp tonight on the Sanwight side and be ready to cross in the morning. We've managed to muster not only the regular army, but also a large group of the fishermen who are eager to see the end of the dragons. With the dragons gone, the dolphins will soon be eliminated. I believe you'll be pleased. We have over five thousand foot soldiers, more than I would've imagined. They may not all be trained, but they know what to do with their fists. I think they'll be able to overcome the small resistance Draconia will mount."

"Excellent! That's very good news. It's a much larger force than I could've hoped for," said the Baron. "My men will join you immediately, I'll be at the encampment later. I need to meet with King Stefan first and apprise him of the changes. You may go."

The Baron made his way to the Palace. He hoped he wasn't going to have trouble with King Stefan over the betrothal. When he arrived at the Palace he was immediately shown in to the King's council chambers.

"Welcome, Baron," said King Stefan. "How are our plans progressing?"

"Very well indeed," replied the Baron smoothly. "There've been just a few minor changes, which I need to apprise you of, sire."

"Certainly," said King Stefan. "I heard talk of some incident during the night? Was that connected with you?"

"Yes," said the Baron. He proceeded to update King Stefan on the kidnapping and rescue of Prince Rupert. The Baron made sure he downplayed the kidnapping.

"What?" roared the King, "You kidnapped an *innocent child?* I want *no* part in such actions!"

"The boy was not harmed in the *least,* your majesty," replied the Baron. "King Jacob would never agree to banishment or punishment of dragons unless we had some sort of *hold* over him. I did it before we had formed our alliance, but now that I have your backing and enough men to invade Draconia, it won't be necessary to resort to such *disgusting* tactics. I agree that they're not an honorable way to conduct a takeover and I'm very glad that Prince Rupert is *safely* back home. It's all worked out just fine. Now we're ready to mount our invasion tomorrow morning."

"Well," said King Stefan, clearly unsure. "I guess that's all right...and when will we announce the betrothal of Gregory and Priscilla? Before or after the invasion?"

"That's the other *slight* change," answered the Baron. "Gregory has defected. He's betrayed me and is helping the dragon riders. I've decided he won't be a suitable husband for Priscilla."

"What do you have in mind instead?" asked King Stefan. "Your other son? Lance?"

"No," replied the Baron, feeling slightly uneasy, but keeping his face a mask of calm assurance. "Lance has refused to be part of the invasion as well—although he has assured me that he won't help King Jacob. I think it would be best if I married Priscilla myself. This way, she'll be queen *immediately.* It'll be a much stronger bond between our kingdoms. We'll be able to move forward immediately with the killing of the dragons and the use of fishing nets against the dolphins. Hopefully, after we have consolidated our alliance we can then move against the gryphons and unicorns shortly after." The Baron moved right into the topic of the genocide, since he knew that was very important to King Stefan. He hoped his marriage proposal wouldn't matter as much as the death of the dragons.

The Baron wanted power. That's why he wanted to eliminate all telepathic beings. It was a power he didn't have. However, King Stefan got *rabid* when he thought about the telepathic bonds—things he considered to be unnatural. The Baron knew that the way to control King Stefan was to play on his fear of the differences and his hatred of the telepathic creatures.

"I'm not very happy about this," said King Stefan. "You're so much *older* than Priscilla."

"But, sire, I will love and protect her in ways that my sons never could've. I have experience and knowledge of women that will make me a kind and sympathetic husband," replied the Baron, his tone soft and gentle.

"I suppose," agreed King Stefan twisting his hands. "It *is* true that we need to get rid of these *creatures.* Their abilities are unnatural, dare I say, *evil.* I've never been able to convince my people of that. Now I have the chance to eliminate the dolphins *only* because the fishermen have gotten greedy. They hate the dolphins because they can't use their nets, but they don't realize how unnatural beings like them can poison their souls."

"I agree, sire," said the Baron firmly and quickly, "and once the dragons are gone, you can lift the ban on the fishing nets and your dolphins will leave or be killed also. Our problems will be solved."

"So you say," said King Stefan. "I just hope you're right and that there'll be no more disruptions. Let's announce the betrothal tonight before the army marches."

"As you wish, sire." The Baron smiled and bowed low. "Now, I must ride for camp. I take it you and Priscilla will come out this evening to wish us success? We can announce the betrothal then."

"Yes, that will be fine," answered King Stefan. "I'll prepare Priscilla for the announcement. I wish her mother could have been here to see this. We were always on the same page...however, Priscilla is a good and obedient daughter. I've raised her to believe in the evilness of magical creatures as well. She'll be a staunch supporter of your plans. We'll see you this evening at camp. Thank you. I look forward to our long and strong alliance."

"As do I, your majesty," replied the Baron. "Until tonight, then." He turned and left.

— 20 —

HOPELESSLY OUTNUMBERED

Hans posted lookouts at the Sanwight end of the pass. They reported back that the Sanwight army was making camp about a mile from the opening.

"How many men are they mustering?" asked Hans when the dragon riders assembled for their evening meeting.

"It looks to be over five thousand on foot, plus the Baron and the Sanwight nobles on horseback—about three hundred," answered Roger, who had been on the latest scouting trip.

"Gads!" Hans covered his eyes. "I had no idea that they would have so many! Even with our barricades and the narrowness of the pass, we're hopelessly outnumbered. We'll give them a good fight, though. The King's men will be here before dawn."

Emily spoke up. "What about getting help from Forbury and Granvale? What the Baron is planning will eventually affect them as well. If they can assist us now and stop this before it gets a strong foothold in *our* world then we'll all be better off."

"You're right," said Hans. "The Baron is just after power, but King Stefan has always been a bigot. Between the two of them I'm sure they'll try to rid our world of *all* telepathic relationships."

"I can fly to Forbury tonight and try to convince the gryphon riders to join us. Our ambassadors have already been keeping King Alfred informed about the situation. He's put his gryphons and riders on emergency standby. I don't think it'll take a lot to get them moving. With any luck, I should be able to bring reinforcements by midday tomorrow. It's lucky that this pass is very close to the Forbury border as well," Emily said.

"Right," said Hans. "Get on your way as quickly as possible. The Baron's army will attack tomorrow morning, but we can contain them for a while."

Anne spoke up too. "Joseph and I have also talked with Benjamin and the other dolphin riders. Benjamin said he'd be willing to get down the coast on his dolphin Horace and ask for help from Granvale. Our ambassadors have prepared the court there also. Queen Penelope is *not* happy with King Stefan. He treats her with great disdain because she's a unicorn rider. I'm sure that Benjamin can convince them that we need help *urgently.* I believe she's also put her unicorns and riders on standby."

"Excellent," said Hans. "That makes things look much better. OK, Anne, contact Benjamin and get him on his way. Emily, I want you and Esmeralda in the air now."

"Right!" Anne and Emily replied together. They both ran to their respective dragons and departed.

"The rest of you, listen up," said Hans. "The King's men will be here some time during the night. Roger spotted them just a few miles away. As soon as they get here, show them where to make camp and get them hot food. They'll be exhausted, but we need them to be ready to fight in the morning."

"I'll take care of that," replied Roger, one of the oldest riders under Hans's command. "I've worked with most of those Palace guards over the years. They're good men."

Meanwhile, back at Havenshold, Clotilda was gathering her own intelligence and making further plans.

"I don't think we can rely on having *just* those thirteen dragon riders to defend the pass," Clotilda said to the evening rider gathering. "I've just learned from Fire Dancer that the invading army is *much* larger than we anticipated. We need to assist them."

Jake asked, "What else are Hans's riders doing?"

"Emily and Esmeralda are flying to Forbury to ask for assistance from the gryphon riders. I've had William and Thunder alert our ambassadors in Forbury to the current situation, so King Alfred will already have his riders ready to go as soon as Emily and Esmeralda get there. With any luck, they should be back to the pass by tomorrow afternoon," answered Clotilda.

"William has also made contact with the Granvale ambassadors, so they're ready to move. Benjamin is heading their way. Both of our neighboring nations will be ready to support us, but they can't act officially unless we want an all out war. We're calling this a "civil uproar" rather than a "Sanwight invasion." After all, our Baron Geldsmith is leading it. He just has Sanwight nobles with too much time on their hands and disgruntled greedy Sanwight fishermen on his side. Officially, King Stefan hasn't gotten involved, although there are rumors that he is betrothing his eldest daughter to the Baron this evening."

"What?" asked Gregory rather loudly. He and Sylvester had been helping prepare the Havenshold defenses. He was also working on cutting off the volcanic energies to his father's lands. "He's to marry a twelve-year-old? That's obscene!"

"Unfortunately," said Clotilda. "I expect the rumor is true, since I can't think that King Stefan would be stupid enough to let the Baron have all those forces without *some* assurances that he would get the Baron's help in return. King Stefan sees all rider bonds as unnatural. I know he wants to get rid of his own dolphins, not understanding how much they do for him and his people. I can see how the alliance formed between King Stefan and the Baron, each wanting to eliminate something they don't understand and can't control. However, I think poor Stefan has met his match in the Baron. I sure don't envy Priscilla if this marriage takes place, but that's not something we need to discuss today. How can we help Hans further?"

Gregory said, "I think that I need to get up to the pass and try to negotiate with my father. I know that he's angry, but something *has* to be done about him. Sylvester wants to come as well. If we can find a way to disarm the both our fathers then this whole *stupid* invasion would collapse. May we try?"

"That would be wonderful. I hope for all our sakes that you can neutralize both of them," said Clotilda.

Gregory and Sylvester left the hall immediately.

"William, I want you and Thunder to stay in close contact with our ambassadors in Forbury and Granvale. Keep me informed of any developments there. Jake, if Harmony is well enough, can you two head down to the Capitol so that we can keep King Jacob apprised of the latest developments? William and Thunder will keep you and Harmony in the loop."

"Harmony is certainly fit enough to fly that far, and she's very restless, wanting to get back at those who did this to her. We would be honored," replied Jake. "We'll leave within the hour."

"Excellent," concluded Clotilda. "That's if for now. Everyone stay alert."

As soon as Jake and Harmony got to the Capitol they met with King Jacob.

"What's the news?" inquired King Jacob, as he walked into the meeting room.

Jake brought him up-to-date.

King Jacob said, "I can't believe I haven't seen the depths of King Stefan's hatred before. Without Stefan's assistance, the Baron would be nothing more than a nuisance. I suppose he hid it well. He's the only one of the four monarchs who's never had a telepathic bond. That makes him dangerous. The Baron's bad enough, but his motive is easy to understand. He's a bitter, lonely man who lost the only stabilizing influence in his life. Now he has nothing but greed and power to drive him. I think with the right enticements, he could've been dealt with before things got out of hand. This alliance with King Stefan makes that impossible. King Stefan is a maniacal, self-righteous, zealot who feels that he's saving the world. How horrible such hatred is, but his motivations are so deeply rooted that I fear there's no hope for him."

Jake waited respectfully while the King continued. "Thank you, Jake, and all your dragons and riders for saving Rupert, and bringing me back to my senses. I won't let you down again. Now, would you like to share dinner with me and my family before you head back to Havenshold? I know Rupert would love to meet another dragon and rider...if you can bear the attentions of a twelve-year-old boy. He's hoping that he'll be a candidate at the upcoming hatching."

"Certainly, sire." Jake laughed. "It would be our honor."

— 21 —

BETROTHAL AND DECOY

The Baron's forces gathered by nightfall at an encampment a mile away from the pass. The Baron sent a detail of six men into the pass to scout it out as the rest of the army set up camp.

King Stefan and Priscilla arrived just before supper and a makeshift platform was set up with the King's banners on each corner. King Stefan, Priscilla, and Baron Geldsmith stood upon the platform. The rest of the army— the nobles, the fishermen, and the Baron's men—gathered in front.

King Stefan addressed the crowd. "This is a *proud* moment in our history. We are going to begin the *extermination* of the telepaths—those unnatural, foul beings, both human and magical—who distort the *true* order of our world."

Loud cheers went up from the assembled audience. The King continued. "We will take our cause first to Draconia where the dragons and their riders will be eliminated. We're very happy to be uniting with Baron Geldsmith in this *noble* crusade. To that end, and to solidify the ties between our two nations, I am happy to announce the betrothal of my daughter, Priscilla, to Baron Geldsmith."

The army cheered loudly as King Stefan held the Baron's hand in one of his and Priscilla's in the other. The Baron grinned widely and acknowledged the cheers. Priscilla kept her eyes cast down and twisted her handkerchief in her hands. The King said, "Tonight we will feast on foods brought from the Palace for this special occasion." He paused as cheers went wild. "Tomorrow, at dawn, we begin our invasion."

Baron Geldsmith said, "King Stefan, thank you for the enormous honor that you have bestowed upon me by granting me your daughter, Priscilla. I promise I will look after her with tenderness and care. And thank you for joining me in such a *righteous* cause. Together we will rout the dragons out of their lairs and exterminate each and every one! After that, we'll turn to the dolphins, allowing your fishing fleets to use *nets* once again. Draconia and Sanwight will stand *firm* against the evil of telepathy."

The men congratulated themselves enthusiastically and soon everyone was feasting on the delicious fare brought from King Stefan's Palace. As the evening wore on, King Stefan and Priscilla departed for the Palace and the army began to set up the watch and bed down for the night.

Just after midnight, one of the scouts came stumbling back into camp, bloodied and barely alive. The Baron was awakened to take his report. The scout, only just able to speak, said, "Traps, traps. Everywhere. Falling rocks. Everyone else dead. *Crushed,*" He gave a last gasp and slipped into unconsciousness.

The Baron rousted Henry and the Sanwight nobles. "We need another course of action. The pass has been booby-trapped. It'll be treacherous to march the army through it."

"What do you propose then?" asked Terence. "This is the only pass large enough for the army to go through."

"True," said the Baron, "but there is another way in—the way I use when I come to Sanwight. While it's very narrow and won't take the entire army, I don't think it *needs* to. If we can find someone willing to lead a small contingent—say, a hundred men—through to the other side, they'll end up behind the dragon riders. They can then show themselves to the dragon riders and race off toward the Palace. I believe the dragon riders will give chase, thus pulling them *out* of the pass and giving us a safer route."

"And if the decoy squad can move fast enough, they can appear to be storming the Palace to kill King Jacob," announced Terence.

"Yes," said the Baron. "Henry, would you be willing to show Terence the way? Terence, would you be willing to lead this decoy squad?" Both men nodded. "Fine then," said the Baron. "Let's get what sleep we can before dawn. In the morning, Terence, Henry, and all the volunteers you can muster, head for the alternate route. It'll take you most of the morning to get through and out the other side, but you should be on the Draconian side of the pass by midafternoon."

"Sounds about right," said Henry, who knew the route well. "I recommend we take all of our men, as well as fifty horsemen from the Sanwight nobles. We can move faster on horseback."

"I concur," said Terence, giving a nod to Henry.

"I'll command the forces from this side. Now that we know about the rock barricades and traps, we'll move slowly, but deliberately, through the canyon. With any luck, we will be a fourth or third of the way through by the time you appear on the other side and the dragon riders start pursuing you. At that point, we'll be able to move with less caution and will have the dragon riders trapped between us. Good thing the canyon's too narrow for the dragons to fly in and too shallow for them to be safe above us. If they appear above us, we can pick them off like ducks." The Baron laughed.

Just before daybreak, Henry led Terence and the decoy contingent toward the narrow trail. The opening to the trail was covered with brush and brambles. The men swore loudly as they pushed themselves and their horses through the tangles. After about one hundred yards, the brush was less dense and progress was easier. The men mounted their horses and—single file—worked their way through the pass. The trail was very steep and narrow and the horses had to be led in some spots, but Henry reassured the men that they would get out the other side.

Meanwhile, the Baron mustered his forces. "We've received word that the pass is heavily booby-trapped, so move slowly. We have another, smaller force moving in behind to draw off the dragons, so we just need to move forward carefully and confidently."

As soon as the army reached the pass they began to understand the traps. They saw the added boulders and realized that they would be marching in only one or two abreast. With arrows nocked they began to move forward. Out of the corner of his eye, the Baron caught a glimpse of gold high above, but it was gone before he could focus. *Well,* he thought, *they know we are coming now. The battle's finally joined.*

Back at Havenshold, Clotilda was conferring with her remaining riders. "I've been thinking that we should bring King Jacob, Queen Marigold, and Prince Rupert here. The King sent his Palace guard off to help defend the pass, and heaven knows we need everyone there we can manage, but that leaves the royal family vulnerable. If our allies arrive in time, we'll be fine, but if there's a delay, then I don't want the King in a position to be captured.

"They'd be much safer here at Havenshold," Clotilda continued. "I think if we could get a couple stalwart volunteers, that two dragons with riders would be enough to swoop in, take the

King on one and the queen and Rupert on the other, and fly back before anyone in the Capitol is any the wiser. Bernard is wily. He should be able to carry off the deception that they're still at the Palace."

"That's an excellent plan," said Jake. "If I could have William and Thunder go with Harmony and me, we could leave now and bring them back before nightfall."

"Is Harmony up to carrying the extra load?" asked Clotilda.

"She's fully healed, thankfully," said Jake.

Soon, Jake and William were landing in the north courtyard of the Palace—the private courtyard that was used only by the royal family who was having their breakfast.

"What a pleasant surprise," said King Jacob. Rupert jumped up and ran over to meet the dragons. Bernard entered at that moment, having heard the commotion.

"Your Majesty," said Jake. "I come with a request from Clotilda. We would like to fly you and your family to Havenshold until this crisis is past. The bulk of your personal guard isn't here, so you are vulnerable. At Havenshold we could protect you. Everyone at Havenshold is loyal to both you *and* the dragons—something we can't guarantee here at the Palace."

"I concur, your Majesty," said Bernard. "I think you should go."

"Bernard," continued Jake, "Clotilda would like it if you could keep up the pretense that the King is still here. That way any forces that do make it through the pass—we now know that the Baron has assembled an army of over five thousand—"

"What?" interrupted King Jacob. "That many? Are you sure?"

"Yes, sire," said Jake. "We've sent for help from both Forbury and Granvale, but we aren't sure when they will arrive. Anyway, if anyone gets through the pass, they'll head straight for the Palace if they believe you're still here. Bernard, do you think you can manage this?"

Bernard smiled. "It will be my pleasure and honor. I think I can keep people fooled for several days at least."

"Great," said Jake. "But, your Majesties, we must go *now*. The longer we wait, the more likely it is that our deception will be discovered. If we fly out now, anyone seeing us will think we were just messengers. King, you'll ride behind me on Harmony, and Queen Marigold, you and Prince Rupert will ride behind William on Thunder. You'll be covered with capes so that you can't be seen from below."

"I get another dragon ride!" cheered Prince Rupert.

Before five minutes had passed, the royal family was on the dragons and the dragon riders were heading back to Havenshold.

During the ride, Harmony spoke telepathically to King Jacob. *We've missed you, Jacob. We know how hard it was to lose Henrietta, but did you not realize **we** would never leave you alone? You didn't have to carry the burden of her loss by yourself.*

Tears sprang to King Jacob's eyes. *No,* he thought back to her. *I thought I could only talk with Henrietta.*

Well, we've learned a lot more about telepathy since then, said Harmony.

Prince Rupert was thrilled to find out he could communicate with Thunder and they were having a lovely conversation about dragons and spies. Prince Rupert tried to find out if he would be a candidate for the upcoming dragon hatching, but Thunder wouldn't say.

When Thunder spoke telepathically with Queen Marigold, she was terrified at first. Inlike the King, she had never had a telepathic communication with anyone. Thunder was very soothing, and soon she too was enjoying the conversation. She realized that she had always been a little jealous of her husband's relationship with Henrietta, and now she saw that she needn't be.

Telepathy, she thought, *is just talking.*

Before the royal family realized it, they were landing at Havenshold and being greeted by Clotilda. "We are honored to have you staying with us during this crisis," said Clotilda.

"The honor is all ours," replied King Jacob.

— 22 —

BATTLE BEGINS

The Baron gave the signal for his men to move out. Slowly they approached the entrance to the pass. There didn't seem to be anyone around, so they entered two by two. Slowly and carefully—all too aware of the unconscious scout's words just before he lapsed into unconsciousness—they worked there way into the pass, cautiously approaching boulders, wary at any sound—even squirrels hopping from tree to tree above them—wondering how long the pass was.

Hans was feeling reasonably confident. He was most pleased at the way that Anne, Joseph, Samantha, and Spruce had managed to cause a rock slide that had trapped the Baron's scouts. It was a shame that one managed to escape back to the Baron, but on the other hand, maybe that was a good thing. The advancing army would be more cautious. The other five scouts were now tied up in the dragon riders camp and had had their injuries tended to.

That had given Hans a wonderful idea, but he would need the gryphons, unicorns, and their riders to pull it off. He hoped that Emily and Benjamin would succeed in getting help here soon. If it worked, this would not only be the shortest battle in history, but the only one Hans had heard of where there was victory *without* bloodshed.

Hans took advantage of the slow progress of the Baron's army to start putting his plan in action. He needed to be ready once the additional forces arrived. He assembled his riders. "We're going to trap the Baron's army *inside* the pass. We'll block both ends once we have reinforcements, that way they'll be unable to invade and equally unable to retreat."

Anne said, "That is brilliant! How did you come up with that?"

Hans said, "You and Joseph gave me the idea when you handled the scouts so well by causing a rock slide to cut them off. If we can use a rock slide for a few scouts, then we could dynamite the openings to each end of the pass and trap the army *without* killing them."

Hans continued, "I need all of our people to work their way out of the pass. We need to give the Baron something to think about. I need dragons dropping rocks from above, but never quite close enough to hit anyone. That'll also keep the dragons out of the soldiers' arrow range. The Baron will think we're incompetent, but he'll move slowly. After all, I'm sure he thinks he lost five scouts. He doesn't know they were captured."

"Right," said Roger. "We can handle that if some of the younger riders are willing to find us rocks to use as ammunition.."

"Great," answered Hans, with a smile on his face. "Anne and Joseph, can you manage that, since you two weren't here when we moved all the large boulders?"

"Sure thing," replied Anne with only a slight frown. "Roger, we'll have our dragons stay in touch so you will know where your next set of rocks will be."

"Great!" exclaimed Roger.

Roger and his crew headed out. Hans continued. "Fire Dancer will tell Clotilda about our plans. Clotilda can tell Emily that Forbury and Granvale need to bring explosives. I need the rest of you to scope out the pass and see where we should make our blockades. We need to be sure that all the army has entered the pass, but none has exited."

As the dragon riders at the pass were working, Terence and Henry were having a rough, slow passage through the alternate route. So far, they hadn't been detected. They'd decided to make camp at the Baron's ranch and then select the best route to the Draconian side of the pass. They needed to get reasonably close *without* being detected, but not so close that the anticipated pursuit would catch them. With any luck, they'd be at the pass ready to ride for the Capitol by midafternoon.

Back at Havenshold, Clotilda and Matilda had received Hans's report. No one on the side of magical beings wanted to kill anyone. Avoiding bloodshed had not seemed possible, but now Clotilda decided that with swift action on the parts of King Jacob, the governments of Forbury and Granvale, and herself, maybe the battle could be won without death. Clotilda went to meet with King Jacob to apprise him of the plan.

King Jacob said, "This is wonderful. If we can trap the Baron and his army then we can deal with this insurrection where it ought to be handled—the *negotiation* table."

"My thoughts exactly, sire," said Clotilda. "Do I have your permission to contact Emily, Benjamin, and our ambassadors to propose this new plan? It not only has the advantage of a high probability that no one will be killed, but it also will require many fewer troops from Forbury and Granvale."

"By all means," replied King Jacob. "Let's see if maybe we can get in conference with King Alfred and Queen Penelope. This uprising is focused on my throne, but we know there's a much deeper problem—one which will affect our entire world, not just Draconia."

"Most assuredly," answered Clotilda. "Let me contact Emily and Benjamin and set the wheels in motion."

Clotilda explained what was needed. Emily said, *My brother sure is smart. What a wonderful idea. We'll only need a few gryphons and riders at the pass, which means I should be able to get there by **early** afternoon. I wasn't sure I could manage to get a large force there by then, but some explosives and a few riders is no problem.*

Excellent, replied Clotilda. *Please ask King Alfred if he would be willing—once we get the army contained in the pass—to fly in for a negotiation session with King Jacob, Queen Penelope, and King Stefan. Of course, he'll have to be captured first.*

Sure thing, answered Emily. *I feel so much better about this. Killing has never seemed right to me. How clever Anne and Joseph were! I hope we'll be able to convince the Baron—and more importantly King Stefan—that telepathy isn't evil. Today, it will save many lives.*

Definitely, said Clotilda. *Thanks, Emily. I'll leave the Forbury contingent to you. We look forward to your speedy arrival. You'll be responsible for rendezvousing with Hans at the Draconia end of the pass. Benjamin and the unicorn riders from Granvale will have the Sanwight end of the pass. I suspect Benjamin and his dolphin riders will have the added responsibility of capturing King Stefan. I'll talk with you later. Matilda and I need to contact Benjamin and Horace.*

Emily said, *You can count on us. I'll let you know when I have a better idea of our arrival time.*

Emily was off to the court at Forbury. Clotilda and Matilda contacted Anne and Samantha, who acted as a relay to Benjamin and Horace.

How fantastic! announced Benjamin. *Dolphins are peace-loving creatures. They have a connection with the world that makes unnecessary violence abhorrent to them, and while they can go to war if needed for a* **righteous** *cause, the bottom line is that they don't think that war ever solves anything.*

I hear you, replied Clotilda. *Believe me, we* **entirely** *agree. We need you to make contact with the unicorns and their riders and see if you can get a small contingent with demolition experience to block the Sanwight end of the pass.*

That should be no problem, answered Benjamin. *I should be able to have riders at the pass by this afternoon.*

Great, said Clotilda. *If you could, request—once the Baron and his army is contained—that Queen Penelope meet with the other monarchs to negotiate a settlement. Unfortunately, Queen Penelope will not be able to get to the camp through Sanwight. If you could see if she is willing to start riding* **now**—*through Forbury and into Draconia using the longer route, trusting that she will be safe in those lands—by the time she gets near the pass the battle will be over. I'm sure King Alfred will provide her with an escort through Forbury and we will do the same in Draconia.*

Right, said Benjamin. *I'll see what I can do with the help of your ambassadors. So far everyone has shown great eagerness to cooperate and end this battle.*

Clotilda said, *One last thing. I need to ask you to perform one of the hardest, possibly most dangerous, parts of this. We* **need** *to have King Stefan at the negotiating table. Without him, the rest is pointless. We have to stop the power hungry Baron Geldsmith, but a lust for power is no where* **near** *as dangerous as King Stefan's self-righteous hatred. Do you think you could capture him and bring him to the negotiations? If you can get him to the Sanwight side of the pass, I can have Anne and Joseph meet you there and transport you on dragonback to* *the negotiations. That way, we'll have everyone—except the dolphins of course—present. Certainly we can provide transport for more of your riders if that would help.*

Thank you, Clotilda, answered Benjamin, *for your understanding and empathy through all of this. I accept the challenge, on behalf of all dolphin riders, to get King Stefan to the negotiations without* **bloodshed**. *If we all get moving the way I hope we will, I should have him there by late afternoon.*

Thanks, Benjamin, replied Clotilda. *Stay in touch. We will keep you abreast of any further developments as well.*

Clotilda looked at Matilda and said, *Good job, my sweet! I underestimated your telepathic powers. Now, if you aren't too tired, let's update Hans. I think we should send William and Thunder up to the pass to assist with this new plan.*

Matilda smiled. *These riders and dragons of ours are pretty darned smart.*

— 23 —

HAN'S PLAN IN ACTION

Emily was able to meet with King Alfred right after she learned of the new plans. "King Alfred, I've just heard from Clotilda. Things are looking much better. I respectfully request that six of your gryphons and riders—along with some explosives—be allowed to accompany me back to the pass. With any luck, they'll be able to seal the Draconia end of the pass before the Baron's army arrives there. Benjamin is requesting similar assistance from Queen Penelope and the unicorns so that the Sanwight end of the pass may also be sealed, *trapping* the invading army in the middle."

"What a beautiful plan," said King Alfred. "Of course you may have our assistance. Bartholemew is particularly adept with explosives. I'll put him and his gryphon, Drake, in charge of our contingent and have him report to you right away. I know many of my people have been dismayed at what's happening in Draconia. People like King Stefan are dangerous. Unfortunately, he's not alone in his misunderstanding of telepathic powers. Anything Forbury can do to stop the spread of such an insidious disease, we will."

"Thank you, sire," replied Emily gratefully. "I'll be sure that our ambassadors keep you apprised of all actions. Clotilda is hoping that once we have the Baron in custody, that you and Queen Penelope will appear at the negotiation conference to sort this all out. Queen Penelope will have to ride through Forbury to get to the conference, since by then the Sanwight end of the pass she would normally use will be blocked."

"I'd be happy to escort Queen Penelope," answered King Alfred. "I haven't seen her in far too long. It'll be lovely to catch up with her. Please let her know that she and her unicorn, Jerome, will be most welcome here. They can await the end of the battle here in comfort and safety."

"You are *most* gracious, sire," said Emily. "I'll be sure she knows. Now, I'll find Bartholemew and arrange our speedy departure."

Emily left the King's presence and located Bartholemew, who had heard all the plans and was eager to help. He and Emily discussed the terrain and the possibilities for blocking the entrance. Bartholemew had to rely on Emily's knowledge, since he hadn't actually seen the pass opening, but she was able to describe it in great detail, so he felt confident. He picked five more riders to accompany them. By midafternoon, they were at the pass ready to begin work.

Meanwhile, Benjamin was meeting with Queen Penelope and having similar success. "I can't tell you how much your support means to us—the Sanwight dolphin riders and Draconia," announced Benjamin.

"Well, this problem is going to spread like wildfire if it isn't nipped in the bud," replied Queen Penelope. "I understand you need someone good with explosives?"

"Yes," replied Benjamin. "The opening to the pass on the Sanwight side is very narrow, so that only two men at a time may enter. We are hoping that it won't be too complex to seal it completely."

"I'll send Elizabeth and her unicorn Bright Star to head up our contingent. I'll have five other riders accompany you both. Will that be enough?" asked the Queen.

"I think so," answered Benjamin. "I myself will only be able to accompany Elizabeth and her contingent as far as the Sanwight Capitol, since I need to rally my riders and capture King Stefan. It's the only way we'll be able to get him to the negotiations once the battle is ended."

The Queen said, "My riders know the area well, so that shouldn't be a problem. You have the much harder job."

"Thank you, your Majesty," replied Benjamin. "I know it won't be easy, but King Stefan sent most of his guard with the Baron, as he has no idea that he might be a target. My men have been spying on him for some time now. We've been worried about all the unrest in Sanwight—unrest that Baron Geldsmith capitalized on. I think the fact that all the unrest has been focused on obtaining the throne of Draconia will help us capture King Stefan."

"Your reasoning is sound," said the Queen. "Let's hope it proves accurate. I've heard from King Alfred with a very gracious offer of hospitality for Jerome and me until such time as we can continue on to the negotiations in Draconia. We're heading out immediately. Please, keep us informed."

Benjamin nodded with a slight bow. "I'll find Elizabeth now."

Benjamin discussed the plans with Elizabeth and Bright Star, who assured him that they would be able to manage the blocking of the pass entrance easily.

"After we're done," continued Elizabeth, "we'll come back to see how you're managing. Maybe we'll even be able to help transport King Stefan back to the blocked pass for faster pick up by the dragons."

"Thank you," said Benjamin. "Your offer of reinforcements is greatly appreciated. I'm hoping we'll be able to spirit King

Stefan out of the Palace with minimum fuss, but he's a *very* difficult person. I won't take it for granted that his capture will be easy."

Benjamin, Elizabeth, and Bright Star, and the five other unicorns with riders headed out. By midafternoon, Benjamin was at the Palace, having devised a capture plan with his fellow dolphin riders, and Elizabeth's contingency was at the pass getting prepared.

At the Draconian end of the pass, Emily and Bartholemew were working feverishly to prepare. That end of the pass was currently being monitored by Matthew and his dragon, Rosewind. They were keeping watch to be sure that the Baron's army wasn't too close to the exit. As he was watching, he caught sight of movement outside the pass on the road to the Capitol. He called out to Emily and Esmeralda, "The army got past us!"

Emily looked up from her work and quickly mounted Esmeralda so they could fly by to see what had happened. The entire plan would fall apart if the army, or even part of it, had found another way in. Emily spotted Terence and his small force. She quickly realized they were a ruse. but she couldn't allow them to head for the Capitol. "We need to get them turned around and drive them *into* the pass!" shouted Emily.

"I have the explosives all set to detonate," answered Bartholemew. "If we can get them inside, they'll be trapped."

"Great," said Matthew. "Can we herd them like cattle?"

"If six gryphons and two dragons can't spook them into the pass, then we need to hang up our wings," said Emily. "They may have flaming arrows though, so be alert and quick."

The eight winged creatures swooped down on Terence and his men. They began harassing them the way a sheep dog would move sheep. Terence ordered his men to fire, but the arrows were ineffectual.

Henry hollered at Terence, "We *can't* head into the canyon pass!" But there were no other options. The dragons set fire to the brush on each side of the road just ahead of the invading party. Their horses were so spooked that they wouldn't go forward.

Terence quickly realized that he had no choice. He ordered his men into the pass. "We'll just have to catch up with the Baron at this end and let him know what the opposition is as soon as he leaves the pass."

As soon as Terence and his men had cleared the pass opening, Bartholemew gave the signal for the detonation. There were a series of nine explosions. After the dust cleared, Emily and Bartholemew moved in from the Draconian side to examine the entrance.

"There's no way anyone is going to shift this rock for a very long time," said Emily. "Your explosives were expertly placed, Bartholemew."

"Thanks, Emily," answered Bartholemew, "but this job wasn't that hard. The hard part will come when we try to open the pass again once the negotiations are over."

Emily laughed. "Yeah, not much fun doing a job that you know will have to be undone shortly, is there?"

As the dust cleared, they all looked to the newly blocked canyon. "We'll never get out that way!" said Henry. "We must let the Baron know *right away.* He needs to turn his forces around and head back to Sanwight!"

Just as Henry was making his announcement, they heard the more distant rumble from another series of explosions. "Oh no," said Terence. "That sounds as if it's coming from the other end of the pass. We're trapped."

Henry nodded miserably. "I don't think the Baron is going to be happy at all." He moaned.

Outside both entrances to the canyon pass, sounds of cheering arose. Hans—who had proposed the plan—had Fire Dancer let Clotilda and Matilda know that phase one of the defeat of the Baron had been successfully completed. The Baron and his forces were now neatly captured. It would be up to the other monarchs to work on finding a peaceful solution to this nasty insurrection.

Hans smiled. *It's so satisfying to have plans work out properly,* he thought. *Now we just need to hear that Benjamin has captured King Stefan and all the players will be where we need them.*

— 24 —

KING STEFAN

While others were busy blowing up the two pass entrances, Benjamin and a group of dolphin riders were scoping out King Stefan's Palace. The guards were minimal. Horace spoke telepathically to Benjamin from the bay and told him of a legend that may help them. The legend said there was an underwater grotto in the Palace, because the first kings of Sanwight had also been dolphin riders. Horace and the other dolphins had been searching and had recently found an old grate across what looked like a drainage canal. Several of them had managed to get the grate loose and wondered if Benjamin wanted them to explore.

Benjamin encouraged Horace, but only if there were no risks involved. Horace and a few other dolphins entered the canal. Soon Benjamin and his fellow riders could feel the telepathic connection with the dolphins growing stronger. Before they knew it, Horace was announcing that he was in a beautiful underwater grotto with mosaic walls depicting dolphins and riders. They were inside the Palace.

Even more astounding was the fact that Horace and the other dolphins could *sense* King Stefan inside the Palace. They could feel his thoughts. He was very worried. He hated telepaths. He was afraid, because he'd always had voices in his head, voices he'd tried to block out since he was a small boy, because his father had told him telepaths were evil. Horace reported that King Stefan was driven by the fear that he might be a telepath and he couldn't bear it. He'd always been a good boy and believed what his father told him.

Horace reported that King Stefan was worried that the Baron wouldn't manage to kill the dragons and take over Draconia. Without the help of the Baron, King Stefan didn't feel strong enough to eliminate the dolphins. King Stefan had been the one sewing discontent among both the nobles and the fisherman. He'd spread thoughts of greed and avarice among the fishermen so they would resent not being able to use their nets. Further, he encouraged the younger sons of the nobility to become soldiers and learn to fight, because he knew once he'd gotten the fishermen to kill off the dolphins, he would have an uprising. He thought the fishermen were stupid and gullible. They believed the dolphins were keeping the fish away when in fact it was the exact opposite.

Horace said to Benjamin, *Poor King Stefan. He's a wounded soul. He's been living in fear all his life because of his overbearing, father. King Boris also heard the dolphins' voices, but he denied them. It's been centuries since there's been a dolphin-riding king. Some of the kings lacked telepathic abilities, and those who showed any sign of telepathic powers were quickly teased, ridiculed, and denounced. Over generations, the kings learned that telepathy was a **defect** rather than an **asset**.*

As luck would have it, King Stefan's abilities were very strong, and now he was terrified that he was going mad. Benjamin sent thoughts to Horace. *You must try to reach him, to comfort him, and to get him to find the grotto.*

Horace replied, *I'll try.*

Horace gently sent calming thoughts toward King Stefan. *Stefan, you are wonderful. You have a tremendous ability. You are **loved**.*

Stefan shook himself. *Where did those words come from?* he thought. *No one has ever thought **I** was **wonderful!***

Horace continued, *I do, Stefan, and so will others once your **true** self is uncovered. You've been deeply wounded. It's time now for those wounds to heal. I can help you **if** you'll let me.*

Stefan was terrified. "Who are you?" he shouted, and the guard outside his door came charging in.

The guard said, "Are you all right, sire? I heard you shout."

King Stefan realized he had shouted aloud. "No, I'm fine. Just a nightmare. I must have dozed off."

The guard nodded and left the room.

Horace spoke again to Stefan, *You know that your father told you all those things because he **also** was living in fear. He'd been told that telepathy was evil. He was trying to beat it out of you, to make you tough, to help you survive. He didn't know he was wrong.*

What do you mean? thought Stefan, *My father was a great King and a strong man. He knew what he was saying.*

Horace asked, *Did you never wonder at the way your father acted toward the dolphin riders? Did you never wonder why your father avoided going down to the water?*

Stefan replied, *He always said the sea made him sick and he couldn't stand the smell of fish. He had an allergy.*

Horace said, *I think you have lived with this programming for too many years. Your fears are now driving you to hurt your nation. Are you willing to confront your fears?*

I don't know, said Stefan. *How do I know you're real? Maybe I'm going crazy!*

Did you know there is an underwater grotto in the basement of your castle? thought Horace.

No, how could that be? answered Stefan.

Search it out, suggested Horace.

Stefan decided that he would look for some evidence about what he was hearing in his own head. He would explore his castle, something he hadn't done since he was a boy. He knew of many secret passages leading from the King's bedroom. He'd played here when his father ruled. Some of the passages went to other rooms—such as the queen's bedroom or the nursery—but he had a vague memory of another passage that he'd started to explore, but his father had gotten angry and forbidden him to go further. His father even added a door with a lock so that Stefan never found out where it went.

Horace prodded Stefan's thoughts with the question. *Want to find out now what you were forbidden to see?*

Stefan did. He miserable and not a very good King. Something had to change. This war to help the Baron destroy dragons had caused him *anguish.* He knew he was acting irrationally, but he couldn't help it. He was so driven by the fears his father had instilled in him, and what was worse, he was passing those fears onto his sweet Priscilla. He suspected that she also heard the voices. If they were both telepathic, did that make them evil? He might be able to believe that about himself, but never about his Priscilla. She was pure, lovely, young, and innocent, and now he had agreed to having her marry *the Baron.* He had nightmares about that. Maybe it was time to try to discover a new reality, a new truth about himself and his world.

Stefan found the door his father had locked. It was *still* locked, but the door wasn't very well built. Stefan thought he'd be able to take it off its hinges if he just got some tools. He remembered seeing a toolbox in his dressing room, left by some workman who was trying to adjust a sticking drawer in his dresser. Stefan retrieved the toolbox and began to attack the locked door. Horace encouraged him. *Good, Stefan.*

It was hard work, especially since Stefan really didn't know what he was doing, but eventually he managed to demolish the door—more by luck than skill. After lighting a lantern, Stefan headed down the passageway he'd *wanted* to explore so many years ago.

It turned and wound downward through several floors until Stefan realized he was below the basement cellar level. He turned a corner. There it was, just as the voice had described it—a grotto with mosaic walls and a very deep pool. In the pool were several dolphins. He couldn't believe it. Was this really true? Had his ancestors been dolphin riders? What had gone wrong?

He walked to the water's edge. Horace and the others came over. Stefan discovered that the sides of the pool were steep and straight so that the dolphins could come right up to the edge. At first Stefan was hesitant to touch Horace, but Horace encouraged him—both with telepathic thoughts and with dolphin speak. Soon, Stefan was in the water with the dolphins.

He couldn't believe how amazing it was. These creatures were no more evil than his Priscilla was. They were good and kind. What had he done? Was the damage unstoppable? Stefan fell into the old patterns of beating himself up for not being good enough, not being smart enough, and so on—just as he had done since boyhood. He began to hate himself.

Horace broke into his thoughts. *Stefan, stop. Of course you thought that in the past. That was how you were raised. That was the reality you were given. But we can make **new** realities. I can tell that you want to do just that. How would it be if you met with my rider, Benjamin?*

Stefan looked up with a start. ***Benjamin** is your rider? Oh, I've made his life so difficult. I tried to have him arrested after I found out that he had been leading the group who freed Prince Rupert. What have I done?*

Horace stopped him again. *That was the old reality. Benjamin will understand. I'll talk with him. Right now, he and his friends are outside the Palace. They'd really like to meet with you and share with you just what's been happening with the Baron and his plan. Will you listen to them?*

Yes, but how can I find him? My guards are all determined to keep everyone out of the Palace, thought Stefan.

Just as there was a secret entrance from the Palace to this grotto, so there is a secret exit into your private garden. You'll be able to let Benjamin in from there. Go and see if I'm not right, suggested Horace.

Stefan all but ran to the side of the grotto where there was a door. He pushed it open with difficulty. It hadn't been opened in a very long time. He walked into a tunnel that led up to ground level where he saw another gate—one he had never noticed before—which took him into his own private garden. As he shut the gate from the garden side, he noticed that it fit seamlessly into the wall and appeared to be part of the wall. Now that he knew it was there, he would never mistake it for only wall again. He went over to the gate that lead out of his private garden into the main Palace grounds and was surprised to find a group of dolphin riders on the other side.

Benjamin quickly said, "Good evening, sire. We've heard everything from Horace. We want to assure you that we've always been and will always be your faithful servants."

King Stefan bowed his head and wrung his hands. "I'm afraid I haven't been as good a King as you have been servants, but I'm hoping it isn't too late to change all that. I can't believe I believed everything my father said."

"No time for that now," said Benjamin, hurriedly. "Events are unfolding quickly. You know where your truth lies now, and that's all that matters. We can sort out the rest later. I need to let you know that the Baron and his army have been *safely* trapped in the canyon pass with no casualties. The dragons and their riders—aided by both gryphons from Forbury and unicorns from Granvale—have managed that. Now there's to be a negotiation conference at the dragon rider's camp above the pass. King Alfred and Queen Penelope are headed that way now. We need to get you there. Are you willing?"

"Yes," said King Stefan. "I need to undo the damage I've done. But, who will believe me? I can hardly believe it myself. All these years of not realizing *I* was *telepathic.*"

Benjamin smiled. "Don't worry, sire. That's the wonderful thing about telepathy—you can't lie in your own head. Horace saw the truth of *who* you were and helped you to realize it. The other magical creatures will be able to do the same—if you allow them into your mind. You may not realize it yet, but you *can* block them. You've been doing that unconsciously for years. It was only recently—I suspect because of your allowing the Baron to become betrothed to your Priscilla—that your despair reached a point where the unconscious barriers fell. You were crying out for help—loudly—which allowed Horace to find you."

"Amazing," said King Stefan. "I'll attend the negotiations, but how am I to get there?"

"Not to worry," said Benjamin. "We'll escort you out of the grounds where we'll meet some unicorns who've already been able to hear your thoughts. They'll give you a ride to the pass on the Sanwight side. Since that pass is now blocked, you'll then ride dragonback to the plain where the conference will be held. You'll have the opportunity to communicate, not only with your own dolphins, but with unicorns and dragons as well. By tomorrow you may even have chatted with a gryphons or two. Your telepathic abilities are unusually strong—otherwise, your cries for help would never have been heard."

"It is all so strange and more than a little intimidating," replied Stefan. "But, I'm too used to living in fear. At least the *current* fears are more positive—if such a thing can be said about fear—than what I've been under for most of my life. Lead on, Benjamin, and I'll follow you to my next adventure."

— 25 —

BARON GELDSMITH

Meanwhile, back at the pass, Hans looked down at the Baron and his army. Terence's contingent had met up with the Baron and the rest of the force.

Hans debated his next move. He knew that it was important to work with the Baron and to allow the Baron to save face or else they would have to kill or incarcerate him. They just how to figure out how to get the Baron to work with them.

Hans asked Gregory to meet with him. The two of them sat down over tea to discuss the situation. Hans said, "I thank you for coming here to discuss your father's situation. We have him neatly cornered, but I don't know how we want to proceed from here. He's proven himself to be very dangerous. Unless we can find some way to restructure his way of thinking, we're going to have to kill or incarcerate him. He's too dangerous to let loose and I don't know what sort of guarantees from him we could even trust. Ideas?"

"I've been giving this some serious thought," replied Gregory. "Before my mother died, my father was a very different man. He loved her beyond all belief. With her influence he was good and kind. I believe that somewhere inside, *that* man still lives. Since my mother died, when I was six, my father's never allowed her to be spoken of. All pictures of her have been stored away. Worst of all, my father's driven himself to become more and more powerful, gaining riches beyond measure. This latest gambit is just the worst in a long series of horrific events."

"I see," said Hans. "Do you think it's hopeless?"

"I honestly don't know," said Gregory. "I think the first step has to be a meeting with Lance, my father, and me. Lance and I—each in our own way—have tried to compensate for my father's loss, ignoring the fact that we were *also* suffering. Lance, I suspect, blames himself for her death. He's always tried to be a very *dutiful* son and has followed my father's *every* command. Even the charade with the fake dragon was something Lance did because Father asked him to. Like me, Lance loves the dragons, but he also never wanted to be a dragon rider. He's a born baron in the best sense of the word. Taking care of Father's holdings is all he ever wanted. Of course, Father keeps insisting *I'm* the heir, but now I think it's time for the three of us to speak some honest truths to each other. Could you arrange that?"

"Yes," said Hans. "The Baron has a lot of talents that Draconia could use if they were channeled properly. I would like to find a way out of this conundrum *without* bloodshed. I'll have Emily and Esmeralda fly to your castle and let Lance know that he's needed here. Would you like to compose a note to your brother so that he knows that he's safe with them?"

Gregory said, "I can have the note ready in a couple minutes. We have a code so that we know if messages are genuine or not."

"While you're doing that, I'll brief Emily and Esmeralda. Come over as soon as you have the note," replied Hans as he turned to find Emily.

Emily was very happy to be sent on a mission. She and Esmeralda were feeling a bit useless with nothing to do. As soon as Hans explained what she was to do, she agreed. "I've always had a soft spot for Lance...maybe because he is Gregory's brother." She blushed. "We'll be happy to bring him back here. We should be able to have him here in an hour or so."

Gregory arrived with the sealed note for Lance. "Thanks for being willing to do this, and thanks, Esmeralda, for your graciousness in ferrying an extra passenger," said Gregory. "You're both real friends."

Emily blushed as she replied, "Happy to do it, Gregory. Lance will be here before you know it." She and Esmeralda took flight.

"Now for the hard part," said Hans. "We have to convince the Baron to meet. It'll take a dragon to get him out of the pass, but I don't want anyone down there shooting at the dragon in the process."

Gregory said, "I expect my father is none to happy with me, but I'd be happy to ride down there and see if I can convince him to come back up without a fight for negotiations. My father's always been a reasonably honorable man about some things. I think he'd respect the flag of truce. Is there a dragon who would accept me as a rider to go fetch him?"

"You just want to have another dragon ride," Hans joked. "Yes, Fire Dancer. She's one of the only dragons agile enough to get into the narrow canyon safely."

"OK, then," answered Gregory. "Let's see if we can do it."

Good as her word, Emily and Esmeralda were back with Lance within the hour. Lance and Gregory hugged and Gregory told him what he was proposing. Lance agreed it was worth a try. "Don't forget how stubborn Father can be though," cautioned Lance.

Emily laughed. "All you Geldsmith men can be pretty stubborn." Both Lance and Gregory had the good graces to look abashed, looking at their shoes and turning red in the face.

"OK," said Gregory. "I'll go down for Father."

Lance held up his hand. "Sorry, big brother, but Father is *angered* by your actions. He's called you a traitor and told his men they're free to shoot you at will. I'll ride Fire Dancer—if she'll have me," he said, looking at Hans.

Hans agreed. Soon Lance was riding Fire Dancer down into the canyon pass, waving the truce flag.

The Baron could be heard shouting, "Don't shoot! That's Lance!"

Lance had been told not to get off Fire Dancer under any circumstances, for both their safety's sake. He called down to his father. "Father, will you come with me—under the flag of truce—to talk about *solutions* to this crisis? I promise you, you may return to your men at any time and no one will harm your men in your absence. So far, not a single life has been lost and we'd just as soon keep it that way."

"What do you mean—" his father roared, "—that no lives have been lost? What about my scouts—five of them—crushed in an avalanche? Don't those deaths *count?*"

"Father, as you will be able to see for yourself, they *weren't* killed," replied Lance. "They were caught on the wrong side of the avalanche and were rescued by the dragon riders. They're at the camp perfectly safe."

The Baron muttered. "Henry, you're in charge. If I'm not back in an hour, take whatever actions you deem appropriate." The Baron climbed up on Fire Dancer and away they flew.

As they landed in the dragon rider's camp, the Baron looked around and was surprised to see gryphons. *That's why we were defeated,* he thought. He was astonished to hear a voice in his head.

*Yes, Baron, we did indeed help send your forces **back** into the pass, and then barricade the Draconian end. It was the unicorns who sealed off the other end, however—credit where credit is due.*

"Who's that talking at me?" yelled the Baron and looked around. Drake stepped forward and looked the Baron in the eyes.

Did you not know you had telepathic abilities? he thought at the Baron. The Baron was now totally flustered.

"No, of course not," he answered aloud.

"No, of course not what, Father?" asked Lance.

"That gryphon is in my head!" roared the Baron. "Get him out of here."

Hans quickly moved to talk with Bartholemew and Drake, and they stepped back from the group. Hans addressed the Baron, "We'd like to see if there's a way we can work things out so that there's peace again. Lance and Gregory said that they thought a family meeting was overdue, so if you'll step this way, Baron, you and your sons may meet in the privacy of my tent."

"I don't have anything to say to that *traitor* who calls himself my son," the Baron said. "I'm beginning to wonder about *this* one also," he added as he pointed to Lance.

"*Please,* Father," pleaded Lance. "Haven't things gone on long enough? We've *needed* to talk for years. Now we have the opportunity to see if we can find any resolution for the pain that dominates *all* our lives."

"I'm not promising anything," grumbled the Baron, but he followed Lance to Hans's tent where they found Gregory waiting.

Gregory rose as his father entered the tent, then bowed on one knee. "Please forgive me, Father, but I just couldn't support you in this last plot, though I love you."

The Baron motioned for him to stand and the three of them found seats around a table. The Baron said, "You have a very funny way of *showing* your love. At least Lance did what I *told* him."

"But Father," interrupted Lance, "It was *wrong*. I *only* did it to make it up to you for *killing mother!*"

The Baron looked horrified. "What? You didn't kill her! What utter rubbish."

"She died giving birth to *me,*" continued Lance. "Without me, she would still be alive."

"If you're going to say that," argued his father, "then I share in the blame. She wouldn't have given birth to you if it weren't for me." The Baron's face contorted. "The doctors told me after Gregory was born that she wasn't strong enough to have another child, that as long as she didn't get pregnant again she would live a full and complete life." The Baron wrung his hands in anguish. "I *knew* that, but she knew how much I wanted a second son. What do they call it—an heir and a spare? She insisted that the doctor's were worriers and that she'd be just fine. I shouldn't have believed her, but I wanted another child. Lance, you've been more than I could *ever* hope for."

"But the price was *too high,*" said Lance. "We lost *you* as well as mother."

The Baron looked very hurt. "You didn't lose me. I've been here..."

Lance looked uncomfortably at Gregory, who finally spoke. "Father...you *changed* after Mother's death. You used to be kind. I can remember that from my earliest memories. I saw how you just retreated. I know now why, but at the time I could only think that *I'd* done something horrible wrong. So I tried, father—*really* I did—to be the son you wanted, just as Lance has. Both of us have grown up under this burden of trying to make your life full. It would have been different if you had talked about her, but you didn't. Neither Lance nor I know *anything* about her. I have a few memories that I've tried to share with Lance, but that isn't enough. No pictures of her, no mention of her, and then you retreating into your world of business and power. Do you wonder that we said we lost *you* as well?"

The Baron looked at his sons with a thoughtful expression, as if he were just now realizing they were grown. "Well, you had everything you ever needed," defended the Baron. "I saw to that and you're both now fine, strong men. What are you complaining about?"

"Don't you see, Father? You gave us everything except the one thing we really needed. *Your love,*" replied Lance.

"And truthfully, you don't *know* either of us," continued Gregory. "You only know how you want to *use* us. You wanted me to marry a twelve-year-old princess so you could have a throne. Did you ever ask me what *I* wanted? You married mother out of love. Don't Lance and I deserve the same chance?"

"But—" spluttered the Baron, "—the only girl you've ever showed any interest in is that *dragon* rider. They *can't* be trusted."

"Emily, Father. Her name is Emily," replied Gregory calmly. "I'd trust my life with any dragon *or* rider for that matter. You think because you can't talk telepathically with them that they aren't trustworthy, but that's just your old *shame* rising up— shame that you think you weren't good enough to be picked and neither were your sons. Do you even realize that neither Lance nor I *wanted* to be dragon riders? It wasn't because we weren't good enough. It was because we chose not to be."

"What?" asked the astonished Baron. "Why wouldn't you want to be a rider? I *always* did!"

"That's the point," said Lance. "You've never taken the time to get to know either of us. Your dreams are wonderful for you, but they're not ours. We have to be true to what we want. We've tried to do this in our own ways without hurting you, but your actions have forced both of us to take a stand against you. It hurts more than we can say."

"Father, can't you remember what things were like when mother was alive? What you were like?" asked Gregory. "You and Mother grew up together and your love deepened. You were disappointed that as a new arrival in Draconia you weren't selected as a candidate for the dragon hatching, but can't you see that the dragons didn't even *know* you? You hadn't proven yourself in love for Mother since you both were still so young or in love for Draconia. Mother told you this, I know, and you tried to convince yourself that it would be enough to have dragon riders for *sons*—"

"My father was a rider," said the Baron. "I've never shared this with anyone except your mother, who kept my secret. He was a gryphon rider...he and his gryphon were killed in a mining accident. My mother couldn't live without him and she wasted away. I was raised by my father's uncle, who was a gem trader. I fell in love with your mother at first sight and I *knew* she was the right girl for me. My uncle really wasn't suited to raising kids, so he happily accepted your grandfather's offer. I left before I could have become a gryphon rider and I wasn't here long enough to be a dragon rider. As long as I had your mother though, none of that mattered...but when she died, I became a very *bitter* old man. Now I've alienated you both."

"No, Father," said Lance and Gregory in unison.

Gregory continued, "We love you, but you have to put *aside* your bitterness. You're a strong man with a lot of talent, and there's a lot of good you could do for Draconia. Or you could see about a life in Forbury, where you grew up, if you prefer. That gryphon spoke to you, even if you didn't understand that you *had* that power."

"There are still options," said Lance. "Though, you're going to have to make atonement for all the damage you've done—thankfully, no lives have been lost and Prince Rupert seems none the worse for his adventure—but restitution must be made. All four monarchs will be meeting soon to discuss your fate, King Stefan's fate, and King Jacob's, since he didn't handle the kidnapping of Rupert as a monarch ought."

"Whatever happens, it'll be up to *you* to prove that you're penitent and convince them of the genuineness of your remorse," said Gregory. "But please know that Lance and I *love* you. We want to be able to work this out."

The Baron looked thoughtful as he replied. "I'll throw myself on the mercy of King Jacob, and I'll ask for protection for my men. I'll take whatever punishment is meted out to me, as long as I know I haven't lost you two."

Lance and Gregory embraced their father and then went out to let Hans know that their father was coming around.

— 26 —

THE GATHERING

Baron Geldsmith gave his word that he wouldn't try to escape and stayed in the dragon riders' camp. First, he asked Lance to take him back down to his men so that he could assure Henry and the others that things would be worked out. Henry was most relieved to see him. "So glad you're back, Baron," Henry said.

"I'm going to go back up and spend the evening with my sons, Henry, but I wanted to let you know that a lot has happened, and it's all good. While we'll have to make some restitutions for the damage we've done, things will work out. I'll make sure that you and our men are not part of the repercussions. Rest easy tonight and tell the men to do the same. Tomorrow should bring the dawn of a new world for us all," answered the Baron.

"Are you sure?" asked Henry. "You don't sound like yourself."

"That's just it, Henry," replied the Baron. "Thanks to my sons, I'm starting to find the self I lost when Catherine died. Don't worry. Everything will work out and I'll do right by you. Never fear. Now, have a good night and I'll talk with you further tomorrow when I know more. Believe me, I appreciate how you have supported me over the years. That loyalty will not go unrewarded."

"Thank you, Baron," answered a very puzzled Henry.

The Baron got back on Fire Dancer with Lance, and Fire Dancer took them out of the canyon pass. The Baron spent the evening talking with his sons. They shared as they had never done.

Gregory admitted that he didn't want to be the heir to the estate and that Lance would do a much better job of it. "I want to be a volcanologist. Do you know that at the moment, especially after we diverted the power from your lands in retaliation for the blockade, that the volcano is getting closer and closer to a *real* eruption?"

"No," admitted his father. "I honestly have no idea how volcanoes operate. Certainly I didn't intend to have anything like that happen. I fully admit that I wanted power, but not at the expense of our *world.*"

Gregory said, "The point is that I want to be a scientist, not a landowner. Lance knows all about cattle and sheep. You would be amazed at how much he's learned already from you and Henry. I know he's only eighteen, but he's the one who's best suited to run your lands for you."

"Thanks, brother," said Lance. "I had no idea you were watching me. Father, I really do want to help you run our estate."

"It seems that none of us was really aware of what the other two were doing," said the Baron. "I feel as if I've let the two of you down."

"It's never too late—" said Gregory, "—for us to become a *proper* family. Let's hope that we're allowed that chance after the powers that be decide what to do with you, Father. In any case, while we didn't communicate very well on a lot of levels, you provided us both with solid educations."

"Yeah," agreed Lance. "Until the last year or so things were normal. Both Gregory and I reached our limits and wouldn't follow you to the ends of your efforts, so you must have done *something* right."

"You boys are so like your mother," said the Baron with tears streaming down his face. "We'd better call it a night now. I suspect that tomorrow will be a long day for us all."

Shortly after dawn the next day, King Jacob and Clotilda arrived on Matilda. A few hours later, King Alfred, with Queen Penelope sitting behind him, flew in on Frederick.

Elizabeth and Jerome had returned to Sanwight after sealing the Sanwight entrance to the pass. They met Benjamin and King Stefan outside the Palace. Benjamin told them all that King Stefan had learned. Elizabeth and Jerome were very pleased. They were most happy to be able to transport King Stefan. Benjamin accompanied them on horseback. While they were riding to the blocked pass entrance, Jerome communicated telepathically with King Stefan. Elizabeth and Jerome would be able to testify on King Stefan's behalf as to the changes that were taking place within his psyche.

When they reached the pass, they found Anne and Joseph with Samantha and Spruce. It was decided after Elizabeth and Benjamin reported the developments that Anne and Joseph would continue along with King Stefan while Elizabeth, Jerome, and Benjamin returned to Sanwight to keep order while the decisions concerning King Stefan and the Baron were made.

Sanwight had been ripe for insurrection before the Baron came into the picture, siphoning off energy for the invasion of Draconia. A large part of the insurrection forces were trapped in the pass and couldn't cause more trouble in Sanwight, but Benjamin felt it was necessary to return to look after Princess Priscilla. Even though she was only twelve, she still deserved to be informed. King Stefan gave Benjamin permission to show Priscilla the grotto and to share with her all that he had learned, so while her father was away, Elizabeth, Jerome, Benjamin, and Horace would help educate the princess in the ways of telepathy.

Benjamin and Elizabeth headed back to the Palace as Anne and Joseph flew off, King Stefan riding on Spruce behind Joseph. Again, King Stefan was exposed to another world as Spruce first and then Samantha talked with him. King Stefan couldn't believe how much of life he'd been missing out on. *How could I have been so blind?* thought King Stefan.

Spruce stepped right in. *Quit beating yourself up, please,* thought Spruce back at him. *You did what you needed to do to survive. You wanted to please your father. It is only natural that you would believe what you were taught. Unfortunately, as Benjamin explained to us, dolphin riders were banished from the court several generations ago by one of your ancestors who was not telepathic. Since that time, each monarch has continued the tradition that telepathy was evil and unnatural. Your grandfather and your father were both raised to suppress their talents, although we don't believe their talents were anything more than minor. But **your** talent is a resurgence of that telepathy-gene. Not only would you have made a spectacular dolphin rider, but your talents allow you to communicate with unicorns, dragons, and I'm sure gryphons as well. That is **extremely** rare. I don't know if you realize just how **lucky** you are."*

To be honest, thought King Stefan to both Spruce and Samantha, *this is overwhelming for me.*

We're very lucky, communicated Samantha, *that the combination of rider and creature is extremely hard to corrupt. You could get a bad rider, but the partner would abandon a corrupt rider. Similarly, if a dragon turned evil, the rider wouldn't support her or him anymore. It's one of the safeguards set up in this* *world of magical creatures. You are most unusual. In most experiences, riders are **only** telepathic with their own magical creature. All of a sudden we're finding exceptions, such as Anne's ability to reach Benjamin and Horace, or William and Thunder's abilities to communicate with most of the other dragons. We'll have to wait to explore that until this present crisis is sorted out.*

Here we are now, and rest assured you aren't going into this meeting alone. I've read your heart—as have Spruce, Jerome, and Horace—and you can't have that many magical creatures reading you and not find the real truth.

The dragons landed and Anne and Joseph escorted King Stefan off to meet with the other monarchs. King Stefan would be interviewed. He knew it'd be hard to convince King Jacob, King Alfred, and Queen Penelope that he'd been deluded and had finally woken up to a better reality, but he was hopeful that he could make amends for his wrongs. All of a sudden life seemed good to him as he walked forth into the gathering.

— 27 —

PEACE NEGOTIATIONS

Once everyone had arrived, King Jacob called the meeting to order inside the large tent provided by the dragon riders. Outside, the wind was howling and there were indications that it soon might be snowing, but thankfully they were not at the mercy of the elements.

King Jacob began. "We're here to decide what to do about the current unrest in two of our nations, and the resultant invasion of Draconia by Baron Geldsmith and an army from Sanwight. First, I wish to recognize my own dragon riders, most especially Hans and Fire Dancer, for stopping the battle without any loss of life."

Cheers and applause followed this statement. King Jacob noticed that both Baron Geldsmith and King Stefan joined in the applause. He took that as a good sign and maybe an indication that the brief heads-up he'd received from Clotilda was in fact true—major changes were happening.

King Jacob continued, "I'd also like to thank both King Alfred and Queen Penelope for their assistance—not only by providing the means to execute Hans's plan, but also for their willingness to attend this meeting." More cheering accompanied these remarks. King Jacob said, "This unfortunate incident has brought to light a number of issues that need to be addressed. It's been years since all four nations have gathered. In fact, it may not have happened since Draconia was established over five hundred years ago. I think is part of our problem."

"Hear, hear," concurred both King Alfred and Queen Penelope.

"As you all may remember from your history lessons," continued King Jacob, "our world is a strange one. Three nations were founded many, many centuries ago and all three have an honorable heritage, but a goodly portion of this world remained uninhabited because of the volcano...until the dragons and dragon riders arrived. We were *happy* to find a land where magical beings were honored—where telepathy existed and was not feared."

King Stefan looked embarrassed. King Jacob quickly continued. "The geography of our nation has isolated us more than anything. Because of the volcano, Draconia has only a narrow pass on its border with Sanwight, an even smaller pass with Forbury, and no land passage with Granvale. Granvale has limited access to both Forbury and Sanwight, but it's not easy. Over the years, the paths that were there have fallen into disrepair and disuse.

"We've kept in touch telepathically, which is to the credit of our magical partners, and they're also willing to transport trade goods. That's why we're still able to get together for the good of our world," finished King Jacob. "We now have to deal with at least *three* issues." There was a murmuring in the crowd. King Jacob held up his hand for silence. "Everyone knows about Baron Geldsmith's treasonous acts and King Stefan's support of him—e'll get to those momentarily. What many of you may not be aware of is my *own* failing in all this."

There was stunned silence. King Jacob continued, "My son, Rupert, was kidnapped shortly after the Dragon Rider graduation ceremony. I was so upset and so concerned for my son's safety, that I allowed myself to be blackmailed by Baron Geldsmith. I let my position as Rupert's father blind me to my greater responsibility to my nation. A king cannot put his family above the welfare of the rest of his people. I'm father to Draconia, and I lost sight of that because of my fears for Rupert. In the end, I proved myself unfit to lead my nation. I wish to abdicate my throne in favor of Clotilda."

Shouts and protests filled the air. King Jacob demanded silence. "Hear me out! I think—as we will discover more and more as the negotiations continue—that our world is best served when the monarchs are active riders. King Alfred has Frederick, and Queen Penelope has Bright Star. Both of these monarchs rule their people wisely and compassionately. Much of Sanwight's discontent stems, as King Stefan himself will shortly testify, from the fact that Sanwight's monarchs have lost *touch* with the dolphins." King Stefan nodded vigorously.

King Jacob continued, "I was once a dragon rider, and I miss my Henrietta tremendously, but I thought since I no longer had my own dragon that I had no abilities to communicate telepathically at all. The dragon riders themselves have stepped forward to show me just how wrong I was, but nevertheless, I do believe that having a dragon and rider as monarch is in Draconia's best interest. Honestly, if my family were threatened again, I could hope I would react differently, but I couldn't promise it. The successful outcome of this entire situation has been possible because of Clotilda and Matilda's leadership. Who knows where any of us would be had we not had that from the beginning. It is entirely to them that I owe the safe return of Prince Rupert. Draconia could not be in better hands. So I now *insist* that Clotilda become Queen of Draconia. I have the right to chose my successor and I exercise that right now."

Clotilda was silent through all this, as her jaw fell open and she started breathing faster, completely thunderstruck. She spoke telepathically with Matilda, *Did you have any idea he was going to do anything so foolish?*

No, I didn't, answered Matilda. *What about Prince Rupert? He's to be selected as a dragon egg candidate. The candidates are to be notified as soon as these proceedings are completed.*

Yes, indeed, said Clotilda. *Of course, Rupert is very young. He hasn't proven himself yet. What do I say, Matilda? They're all staring at me!*

King Jacob is correct. You would make a fine leader, and if Prince Rupert proves that he is a proper heir for his father, you could always do what King Jacob is now doing and abdicate in his favor, thought Matilda.

Clotilda could delay answering no longer. "King Jacob," she said, "you've taken me completely by surprise. I'm very honored. I don't know what to say."

King Jacob smiled. "You'll say, I accept, because I've made this request as your King. I know it is the right choice. You've proven yourself at the time of our greatest peril. You've saved not only Draconia and the dragons, but our entire world."

King Stefan hesitantly asked if he could say something. King Jacob nodded and King Stefan said, "Clotilda, you know what's happened to me when I didn't have Henrietta to help me rule properly. If Henrietta had been at my side, I still would have been terrified for Rupert, but she would have provided a strength and stability to help me see where my true responsibilities lay. Each of our nations *needs* to be governed at the highest level by a magical creature and rider. You have the experience necessary for leadership and you still have a strong and active dragon. The two of you will rule wisely and fairly."

King Alfred stepped in. "Forbury," he said, "has been lucky her monarchs have always been gryphon riders. When the monarch has lost their gryphon, or the gryphon has lost their rider, they've stepped down. It's how we have stayed strong and it's how we've avoided succession issues."

Queen Penelope concurred. "The same has been true in Granvale," she noted. "The reigning monarchs were always a unicorn and rider—paired monarchs—and the loss of one meant that the other would pick a successor and retire."

King Stefan hesitated before speaking. "It may be presumptuous of me to say anything before you all decide what to do with me, but I have already decided that no matter what the outcome, I *will* recommend as strongly as possible that Benjamin and Horace take over in Sanwight. Everything I've heard convinces me further that we need a magical creature and rider pair on all thrones."

"OK!" said Clotilda as she held up her hands in surrender. "Matilda and I accept your kind, if insistent, offer. We'll succeed King Jacob on the throne of Draconia...but Jacob, you are going to be my right hand. You can't just melt away."

Jacob laughed. "I'll be honored to be your right hand, Clotilda. Now, will you please chair the rest of the negotiations as your first act as Queen? Of course, you still have to be crowned officially and there will be major celebrations to endure!"

Clotilda groaned. "Let's get on with these proceedings. You mentioned that there were three items on the agenda. I take it now we've dealt with the first?" she asked.

Jacob smiled and nodded. "As the new ruler of Draconia, you can work with the other nations to bring about decisions that we all can live with. Thank you, Clotilda and Matilda," he concluded, bowing to them both and stepping back into the crowd of riders.

— 28 —

NEGOTIATIONS CONTINUED

"OK, quiet, now," said Clotilda. "I think the next item to be discussed should be King Stefan. It wasn't hard for Baron Geldsmith to draft him into action, but he wasn't the *main* perpetrator, so let's deal with him next. King Stefan, what do you have to say about your part in this whole sorry mess?"

King Stefan stood rigidly and spoke softly but clearly. "I won't make any excuses for my behavior. I was hell-bent on genocide. I wanted all magical creatures wiped from the face of this world. I deserve any punishment you care to mete out." He sat down.

Clotilda was dumbstruck. She'd expected him to plead a change of heart, not take responsibility for his actions.

Before she could say anything, Joseph shouted, "May Anne and I speak? We have important evidence."

Gratefully, Clotilda answered, "Of course."

Anne began, "We were asked by Benjamin and Elizabeth to transport King Stefan here. Benjamin gave me a full report of how they had gotten King Stefan to us. At first, Benjamin and the other dolphin riders assumed they'd have to break into the Palace and kidnap King Stefan to bring him here, but Horace and the other dolphins had another suggestion."

Joseph went on to relate the entire story of the underground grotto, the tale told by the mosaic walls, the way Horace had succeeded in speaking with King Stefan telepathically, and guiding him down to the grotto so he could see the truth for himself, and learn how not only he, but his father before him, and probably his grandfather before that, had all been brought up under a very rigid and false belief system.

Anne continued the saga. "Changing ones beliefs changes one's reality. The world itself is the same, but your vision of it becomes vastly different."

Joseph took over. "We believe that is what's happened to King Stefan, and what he isn't telling you, is how his beliefs have changed."

"King Stefan possesses a unique and powerful telepathic ability," said Anne. "Not only was Horace able to hear King Stefan when he cried out for help, but since opening his mind to Horace, King Stefan has been able to talk telepathically with Elizabeth's Jerome as well as Samantha and Spruce. You know, Clotilda, that William especially has been working on studying telepathy and learning about the ranges and the abilities of all our dragons—even William hasn't talked with dolphins, unicorns, or gryphons." She smiled. "Benjamin and Elizabeth had to go back to the Palace at Sanwight, but they wanted us to add their voices to the plea that we think King Stefan has a really powerful and unique telepathic ability. Now that he realizes how much good can be accomplished through the use of telepathy, we'd like to plead on his behalf for mercy."

William was too excited to sit still. "He can communicate with all *four* magical species telepathically? That's incredible!"

Clotilda laughed. "Hang on, William, you'll get your chance to study this. I promise. I don't believe he's communicated with gryphons."

Bartholemew interrupted. "Drake would be most happy to test it if you like."

While Bartholemew was saying that, Drake was speaking telepathically with King Stefan. *Can you hear me? Do you truly believe in telepathy now? Are you sure you won't decide it is evil and turn on us?*

King Stefan thought back, *I'm honored that you would deign to speak with one such as myself. I have been a blind fool and I am very eager to learn and to make up for my past bigotry and hatred.*

Bartholemew was silent for a minute and then he said, "Drake's just let me know that he also can speak with King Stefan. He *also* believes in the sincerity of King Stefan's heart. The fact that all four magical species vouch for King Stefan says a lot. I don't know of anyone else who could call on such testimony."

"Thank you, one and all, for your support of King Stefan," said Clotilda. "Stefan, what do you have to say about all this? Why didn't you mention it?"

"As you might imagine, the last twenty-four hours have been earthshaking," began King Stefan. "I just always trusted my father. I'm honored and touched by all the support I've been shown by some truly remarkable beings—human and magical. I hope, with help, to turn my life around, but none of that changes what I've done. My country's in chaos because I was too successful in convincing the fishermen that the dolphins were harming their catch, even though I *knew* they were helping it. I encouraged the younger sons of our nobles to become soldiers with the idea of building up an army that could perform genocide. Those acts will be hard to undo. I need to take responsibility for my actions. The fact that I'd been raised to believe untruths does not change my responsibility."

"Stefan," began Clotilda, "even when you were hopelessly misguided, you were doing what you *thought* was right. You've always acted with the highest personal honor code. We're most relieved to discover that you've seen just how wrong your beliefs were. We understand that you'll need help and support to undo the wrongs you've caused, but the fact that you are such a powerful telepath means that you are also a very *important* person to our world."

King Alfred said, "King Stefan, we've had our differences, and we've never been close, but the fact that you cried out for help, that you reached a point where you knew you couldn't continue as you were, that means a lot. Your ability to communicate with all species is a priceless gift that I hope you'll be willing to share with us."

Queen Penelope concurred. "I think that the entire subject of telepathy needs to be researched more. Your William, Clotilda, seems to have begun already. I suggest that we set up a forum for us all to participate in this."

Clotilda nodded. "This latest graduating class surprised me on a number of fronts," she said as she looked proudly at Joseph, Anne, Emily, and William. "I think we'll have a lot to learn from this group.

"As far as King Stefan's punishment goes, I think his change of heart and the realization of who he truly is and what the dolphin rider heritage really means has gone a long way in softening the punishment. However, as you *yourself* said, Stefan, you've done a lot of damage. I support your earlier statement to abdicate the throne in favor of Benjamin and Horace. If I have to be Queen of Draconia, then I want a fellow sufferer, and Benjamin can be King of Sanwight. Furthermore, you'll work with Benjamin to provide an orderly transition, and you'll confess to your subjects the part you played in misleading them. You'll also work with Priscilla and allow Benjamin and Horace to help her discover her own powers. She's still young and so probably has not locked her mind beyond opening. Do you agree to all this?"

King Stefan said, "Yes. You've been most generous with me. I'll even go down into the canyon pass now, if you wish, and speak to my men *directly.*"

"Yes, shortly," said Clotilda. "I suspect both you and the Baron will have words for them. Lastly, I would like you to be part of the forum to study telepathy. I suggest William as the Draconian representative and you for Sanwight. King Alfred and Queen Penelope, you may each suggest your representatives. Agreed?"

Everyone nodded. William positively glowed.

"OK," said Clotilda, "that takes care of point two on the agenda.

— 29 —

NEGOTIATIONS CONCLUDED

Clotilda continued. "We now have one last item to deal with—you, Baron Geldsmith. You started this insurrection in the first place—kidnapping Prince Rupert, blackmailing King Jacob, gaining King Stefan's support, and mounting an invasion. What do you have to say for yourself?"

"Guilty as charged and ready to take whatever punishment you care to give me," replied the Baron.

"Wait!" shouted both Gregory and Lance. Lance said, "We want to speak on our father's behalf."

"No, boys," said the Baron. "I *appreciate* your loyalty, but please stay out of this. I'm guilty."

"We know," said Gregory, "but we also have information that would affect the outcome."

Clotilda held up her hand as the Baron started to speak, "We'll hear what your sons have to say," she said. "Continue, Gregory."

"Once the army was trapped in the canyon pass," began Gregory, "Hans came to me to ask me if I could think of any way to find a solution that would allow those involved to repent without losing too much face. He knew that simply beating up the perpetrators would only anger them and that no matter what the punishment, eventually they would retaliate."

"Is this true, Hans?" asked Clotilda.

"Yes," answered Hans. "The Baron is a *proud* man. He's been driven to seek more and more power. He's also—*I* believe—driven by the shame of never becoming a dragon rider and never having his sons become riders. I asked Gregory what he thought we could do to get out of this predicament. Gregory confirmed what I'd thought about his father and said that he thought it was high time he and Lance talked—heart to heart—with their father. I sent for Lance and have since allowed the three of them to use my tent. I believe very *fruitful* discussions have taken place."

"I see," said Clotilda very thoughtfully. She turned to Lance and Gregory.

"Well," said Lance hesitantly, "none of us had really ever spoken to the other—not about anything that mattered. Neither Gregory nor I ever wanted to be dragon riders, but all these years, my father has believed that the dragons thought *we* weren't good enough. He's harbored that resentment and it has festered. He never had the chance to be a dragon rider or a gryphon rider, because he fell in love with my mother."

"I remember that," said King Alfred. "I was reluctant to give my permission, because the child didn't know that the gryphons had singled him out to be nominated for the gryphon birthing ceremony."

"What?" asked the Baron. "I never knew. My uncle never told me."

"He wouldn't have," continued King Alfred. "He was never happy that he was saddled with you. He wanted to unload you. I should let you know, by the way, that your uncle died last year. His estate—should you get out of this situation relatively intact—is yours. You're the only living heir, but that's for another time."

Gregory took over the testimony. "My father's been living a shame-filled life. I think it's a good thing that neither Lance nor I knew this, as we both tried so hard to please him and to make up for his loss of his wife. We were so worried about doing our best to make our father's world right that we never healed from our own loss."

Lance nodded. "You can imagine that we were a pretty dysfunctional family, but a number of things came together for us yesterday. My father never knew how we felt—that we had no desire to be dragon riders. It had nothing to do with his or our not being good enough. My mother's death was no one's fault—and best of all, my father discovered he has a latent telepathic ability with gryphons. Things have *changed* for our family, and for how our father views telepathic creatures and their importance in the world."

Gregory said, "My father has agreed to my choice of career as volcanologist—by the way, someone should release the energies back to my father's land post haste, as the pressures in the volcano are rising. I want to see what can be done to harness the volcano's power more effectively so all four nations can benefit from added energy, and so there'll be no eruptions that would destroy Draconia and parts of Forbury."

"I understand," said Clotilda. "Someone wise once told me that when people act strangely it behooves us to try to find out *why.* I'm very glad that you two have finally gotten old enough to be able to talk to your father. It's too bad so many had to be hurt before that happened, though.

"Well, Baron, what do you have to say? What are you feeling right now—and be honest, because now that we know that you can speak telepathically gryphons, we'll be able to tell if you're speaking from your heart. Bartholemew, if it's all right with both of you, could you please ask Drake to monitor?"

"Certainly," replied Bartholemew.

The Baron hesitated and then began, "King Stefan said the last twenty-four hours had been earthshaking for him, turning his world on its head and rocking his beliefs to their very foundations. I too have had some pretty hard revelations since I was brought up from the pass. Why my sons don't hate me is beyond me. I see how devastated they were by the death of their mother...I'm not sure how they both managed to grow up to be such fine young men. I just hope that I'll be able to get to know them as they really are and not as I *wanted* to make them be. I was so destroyed by Catherine's death that I failed to see how her death affected us. I closed off my heart and used my talents and resources to try to make up for her loss and *my* deficiencies. I now see how circumstances worked to bring about events that really were not about me at all. I wasn't chosen by a gryphon because I was moving to Draconia. My love for Catherine was a deep and abiding love for us both, but I was so new to Draconia that I was an unknown quantity as far as the dragons were concerned, so of course I wasn't selected."

Clotilda held up her hand. She cocked her head. "Matilda has just informed me that the dragons *did* consider you. First, you didn't seem to have any telepathic ability, but more importantly, they saw that your *true* skill was in people management. They felt you had a career in business. Matilda wanted you to know that it was not because of any *deficiencies* on your part, just different abilities that caused them not to select you."

"Thank you, Clotilda, for letting me know that, and you too, Matilda. It really does mean a lot. I guess we all make assumptions with insufficient data. Anyway, I'm very sorry for all the damage I've done and trouble I've caused, and I *truly* would like to make restitution in whatever way you deem proper. I don't harbor any resentment toward you. I just wish I hadn't been so blind and stupid. My sons have both forgiven me and that's more than I ever hoped."

Clotilda conferred with both King Alfred and Queen Penelope for several minutes. "We've reached our decision. Baron, you will lead the men down in the canyon pass—after both you *and* King Stefan speak to them—in the deconstruction of the blockades. We'll be sure you have plenty of supplies and food, but it *will* be done by hand. Thanks to Gregory's heads-up, we've discovered that the volcano isn't just *unhappy* about the blockage of your power, but the explosions set off to block the pass *disrupted* the plates that the volcano sits on. We don't dare set off any more explosions. You and your men will work with pick axes and you will clear both ends.

"Once that's completed, the men are free to return to their homes and their lives. However, we would then ask you if you would be willing to use your management skills to organize a new company—comprised of people from all four nations—to build better roads and access between nations. Sanwight isn't the only nation with youth in search of adventure, and I think the challenges of building passes and roads around the volcano—without disturbing it—will keep them challenged and gainfully employed for many years. You'll be able to persuade lots of your men, as well as the Sanwight younger nobles, to join such a venture," concluded Clotilda.

King Alfred spoke up, "You now own property in Forbury, and that needs management. It has fallen into disrepair, but I'm sure you'll get your uncle's gem business up and running in no time."

The Baron was too overcome to speak for a few moments. "I'm touched by the faith you have in me. I won't let any of you down. Lance, the homestead is yours. I'll take Henry with me, as I think that would be best for both you *and* him—but you have many very loyal men to guide you if you need help. Gregory,

I shall look forward to discussing volcano dynamics with you. Also, I think Emily is a lovely young lady."

Both Gregory and Emily blushed deeply and then smiled at each other.

"Well, this meeting is over," concluded Clotilda. "Our world is on a very different path, but one that I think will bear fruit for us all. Once the Baron has built us better access, let's be sure we keep in touch on a more *regular* basis. It seems that we'll have a couple coronations in the next few months."

Hans arranged for King Stefan and the Baron to go down into the canyon pass to address their men. The men were very relieved to find out everything had worked out so well and many of them were excited about becoming road engineers.

Hans flew King Stefan back to his Palace so he could abdicate formally to Benjamin, and the Baron talked with Henry and started working out how to unblock the ends of the pass.

— 30 —

EGG HATCHING AGAIN

It was the winter solstice once again and time for another hatching. The last few weeks had been so busy that everyone—except for the dragons—had forgotten about the fact that this year was the triennial hatching year.

True to her word, Matilda had notified the egg candidates right after the peace negotiations ended. One of the happiest candidates was Rupert. His life had been turned around completely when his father abdicated, but his parents were happy. Rupert was in regular school instead of being tutored by private tutors and he loved it. He was starting to make some real friends. His father was happily gardening, whenever Queen Clotilda let him out of the Palace, and his mother had her own kitchen and was thrilled to be able to do her own cooking for her family. All in all, it was much better *not* to be a prince, Rupert had decided, but he couldn't sit still waiting to leave for the hatching. His new friends—David, Sally, Steven, and Hannah, Emily's sister—had also been chosen as candidates. He hoped that all five of them were picked today.

"Can't we leave now?" Rupert wailed to his parents. "I have my dragon's breakfast prepared."

Jacob and Marigold laughed. "Sure, let's head out."

They arrived at the hatching arena and were greeted by Queen Clotilda. "I'm so glad I don't have to oversee *this* at least. The number of Palace functions is way too many," said the Queen, and Marigold nodded in agreement.

"I'm very glad to be out of those, I have to admit," Marigold said.

"Well, *I* have to admit that Hans is doing a first-rate job as dragon leader. It's unusual not to have a purple dragon and rider leading, but Emily's still too inexperienced. I suspect she and Esmeralda are very happy to wait a few years and have her big brother do it instead. But she's learning fast and Hans is proving to be a great teacher," said Clotilda.

Rupert was jiggling all over the place. Clotilda took pity on the anxious boy and said, "I think your friends are around the corner. Would you like to join them?"

"Thanks!" Rupert shouted as he tore off in the direction Clotilda had indicated.

"Doesn't seem that long ago that it was my egg hatching. How about you, Jacob?"

"Yes," he agreed. "Those were *wonderful* days, but I wouldn't trade what I have now for anything," he said as he put his arm around his wife.

"Let's head on in," said Clotilda. "Did you know that Priscilla was chosen by a baby dolphin last week? Her father couldn't be prouder."

"Yes, I heard," said Jacob. "Stefan sent messengers to everyone. It's so wonderful! He seems to be making real progress on the telepathy forum."

"William has incredible reports. We still have *so* much to learn. But I agree, the healing of Stefan is one of the happiest stories we have," said Clotilda.

"Don't forget the Baron," continued Jacob. "Do I see him over there with his sons?"

"Yes," said Clotilda. "That's another happy ending—and there's his gryphon, Oswald. Who ever would have thought that possible?"

"I never did get those details," said Marigold. "How did he bond with a gryphon?"

"Oswald was born last year, but he was lame—missing one wing. Of course, none of the candidates wanted him, and he couldn't find his rider, but the gryphon riders didn't want him killed, so they set up a special nursery for him. The surgeons removed his other wing—he was terribly unbalanced—and that helped him develop more normally. His limp is *nearly* gone. When the Baron finished clearing out the pass, King Alfred invited him for a visit. As part of the tour, Alfred took the Baron to the gryphon sanctuary. The Baron walked into the nursery and was nearly bowled over as Oswald came running at him, shouting telepathically, *"You've come at last!"* There was no arguing with that. The Baron loves Oswald deeply. The Baron isn't keen on heights, so as far as he's concerned, there isn't a better gryphon in the world than Oswald. Another happy ending out of what we all thought was going to be a major tragedy."

"And did I hear—" began Marigold, "—that Gregory has asked Emily to be his wife?"

"Yes." Clotilda chuckled. "After what his father said at the negotiations, Gregory was really put on the spot, but as most of us have suspected for awhile now. Emily cares deeply for him as he does for her. I think it will be a great marriage. Esmeralda is behind it one hundred percent. As you know, Jacob, when a dragon makes up his or her mind, there's no changing it."

Jacob laughed as a hush settled over the crowd. The first egg was beginning to hatch.

Once again, there were thirteen eggs and twenty candidates. For the first time in a number of years, none of the eggs were

Matilda's. Esmeralda had been her last offspring. Surprisingly, Esmeralda had laid an egg this year—newly mated to William's Thunder. Anne's Samantha had mated with Joseph's Spruce, and there was also one of Samantha's eggs in the hatching. It looked as if Anne and Joseph would also be making a match of it. As for William, he was now partnered very happily with Jake.

By the end of the hatching, Clotilda was very happy to see that Rupert had bonded with Esmeralda's purple offspring, Whipper. As usual, the purple was the last to hatch, so not only was Rupert looking very worried, but so were his parents. All four of Rupert's friends had also been chosen. Esmeralda had been right about Emily's sister, Hannah, who had been chosen by the first dragon to hatch—a lovely orange sired by Fire Dancer. Clotilda couldn't help but think back to Emily, William, Anne and Joseph, and wonder if Hans was going to have as many challenges—not to mention as many successes—with this batch of new candidates as she had had with Emily's class. *Life is really fun,* she thought.

ABOUT THE AUTHOR

Daphne Ashling Purpus lives in the Pacific Northwest on Vashon Island with her three dogs and three cats. She volunteers as a tutor and librarian at Student Link—Vashon's alternative high school—and is also an avid quilter, making lap quilts called portable hugs for anyone who needs a hug. She loves to write both poetry and fiction. *Dragon Riders* is her first novel.

Made in the USA
Middletown, DE
26 August 2022

72322403R00126